ONE DEATH,
NINE STORIES

ONE DEATH, NINE STORIES

EDITED BY
Marc Aronson
AND
Charles R. Smith Jr.

CANDLEWICK PRESS

Compilation copyright © 2014 by Marc Aronson and Charles R. Smith Jr.
"Down Below" copyright © 2014 by Rita Williams-Garcia
"Initiation" copyright © 2014 by Ellen Hopkins
"Just Once" copyright © 2014 by A.S. King
"The Next NEXT Level" copyright © 2014 by Torrey Maldonado
"Running Man" copyright © 2014 by Charles R. Smith Jr.
"Making Up the Dead" copyright © 2014 by Nora Raleigh Baskin
"Two-a-Days" copyright © 2014 by Chris Barton
"I Have a Gun" copyright © 2014 by Will Weaver
"Connections" copyright © 2014 by Marina Budhos

First edition 2014

Library of Congress Catalog Card Number 2013957275
ISBN 978-0-7636-5285-2

14 15 16 17 18 19 BVG 10 9 8 7 6 5 4 3 2 1

Printed in Berryville, VA, U.S.A.

This book was typeset in Adobe Garamond.

Candlewick Press
99 Dover Street
Somerville, Massachusetts 02144

visit us at www.candlewick.com

To Charles, for initiating this project
M. A.

Dedicated to Larry and Ricky. Gone too soon.
C. R. S.

DOWN BELOW

RITA WILLIAMS-GARCIA

HERE STANDS MORRIS ADLER at eighteen. Waiting. He found it funny that people said he was a dropout when he hadn't so much dropped as drifted through and then away from school. He had had near-perfect attendance but was never a part of things. Morris Adler. There, but not. Remembers no one and remembered by no one. He wasn't worth the bother to bully or a girl's crush. He took no interests and had no friends. Engaged in no conversations—small talk or meaningful. Neither the prospect of hooking up on the overnight senior trip nor attending prom inspired him to dive into his senior year. Nor did graduation or leaving home for an out-of-state school. Not even the bribe of a five-year-old Honda with new rims moved him to take his road test. It was the last no-show that got him home-tested for smoking weed. "Pee," his mother said. No fuss. No argument. Morris Adler peed in the cup. Unfortunately for his parents, there was no positive result. A positive would have at the very least supplied Mr. and Mrs. Adler with an explanation. Rehab might have earned Morris some status among his peers. *You know Adler? Quiet Adler? Gone celebrity when no one was looking. Adler's in rehab.*

His mother took his lifelessness personally. "Why do you sleep your life away? What have I done?" Even his breathing was a hard sleeper's churn. Sometimes she tapped him hard at the dinner table, thinking he'd fallen asleep while chewing. But he was awake. Staring off into nothing at all.

Morris wasn't aware he was doing it. Breathing like a sleeper with wide-open, unfocused eyes. He just couldn't grab a hold of anything, or nothing grabbed him. So, at the urgings of his mother, who needed to save face at bingo, Morris Adler got his GED and then stood or sat lifelessly around in the house until his uncle Sampson offered him a future.

"I need some low-paying help. Come into the shop tomorrow morning. Eight. Get your life started."

Morris's eyelids might have risen a little higher than usual, but he didn't balk. His mother was pleased, as if a great personal sorrow had been lifted from her. Much to

Mr. Adler's unvoiced objection, she threw an extra lamb chop on her brother Sampson's plate and hummed the chorus to "My Prayer, Divine."

Morris's uncle Sampson, or just Sampson—there were only fourteen years between them—was a good guy. Like Morris, Sampson was a "GED-I Knight." With his limited reserve of interest and energy, Morris sometimes admired his uncle for getting his equivalency diploma and leaving Queens Village to go off to Iraq. Sampson had enlisted in the army to fly helicopters, then came back to the States a mortician.

"We have a pickup," Sampson told him.

Morris found rising at seven to be at work by eight all too early in July, even with a high beam of sun urging him on through sheer bedroom curtains. He wanted to walk the three-quarters of a mile to work, enter the Eternal Rest Funeral Home. Sit down. Look around. Slowly awaken, then begin his work, whatever that entailed. But his uncle was already pushing him out of the entrance before he made it inside. Sampson tilted his head to the parking lot and walked toward the white utility hearse. Morris followed, trailing over to the passenger side.

Sampson said, "Uh-uh," remotely unlocking the doors. He threw his nephew the keys, which Morris failed to catch, and said, "Pick 'em up. Drive."

Morris stopped where he stood, the ring of keys at

the toe of his sneaker. "I don't . . ." He never had followed up with the road test, but he did have his permit.

Neither case concerned Sampson, who had already opened the passenger door and gotten in.

Morris had no choice but to bend down, get the keys. He sighed.

The inside of the utility hearse smelled of lemon car freshener. He sat uncomfortably in the driver's seat before adjusting the rearview mirror.

"This is just one of your tasks," Sampson said. "The real money's at the shop, down below. But," he said, pointing his finger into Morris's shoulder, "you'll need a license for that."

Morris wasn't used to being touched—poked, no less—but he didn't voice his annoyance, nor did he bother to ask about the license. He had no need for money. His parents provided well for him. He didn't go out. Had no girlfriend or prospects to woo and entertain. As a result, his wants were few. He could still feel his uncle's index finger in his shoulder.

Sampson had once told his nephew about his initiation into the mortuary life. Digging mass graves in Iraq. Incinerating remains or collecting exploded remains to ID then ship stateside. He told Morris about things the government didn't want home folks to know. Mr. Adler, Morris's father, sided with the government. He didn't appreciate hearing about his brother-in-law's introduction to the funeral business while they ate dinner. Morris didn't seem to mind, and for a few minutes, he had felt strangely alive while his uncle spoke with color and gusto of his hard, cold initiation over medium-well lamb chops. But Morris could only hang on but for so long, and had soon drifted away, before Sampson had gotten to his days in mortuary school.

Morris turned toward his uncle, an utterance lodged in his throat. He could drive. He had a permit. It had just been a while since he'd gotten behind the wheel of a car.

Sampson shook his head as if to cut off an argument with a speaking person. "Gotta drive for this job. Lots of errands. Pickups. Gotta drive. End of story."

For all of his hesitation, Morris's driving was smooth. They went to the county morgue to pick up the body. Morris stood in the outer hall, guarding the company gurney while Sampson viewed the body and dealt with the paperwork. Together, they received the body within its white plastic bag, a long zipper running in a J from top to end, and strapped it onto their gurney, then pushed it out and loaded it into the utility hearse.

"With reverence," Sampson said as he showed Morris how to push the gurney with the body up the ramp into the hearse. When Morris tried to hand Sampson the keys, Sampson wouldn't take them and slid in on the passenger side. Morris had no choice but to get in on the driver's side.

"A nice, smooth ride," Sampson said, although Morris seemed to possess a smooth, steady hand with the wheel. When they returned to Eternal Rest off of Springfield Boulevard, he and Sampson wheeled the gurney around to the narrow side entrance and pushed it carefully down the ramp, even though the long white plastic sack and its contents had been secured.

"This way," Sampson told Morris, who was at the front of the gurney. "We have to switch."

As awkward as it was to squeeze past Sampson, Morris took a few sideways steps so that he was at the rear of the gurney and Sampson at the head.

Even though Morris didn't need or want an explanation, Sampson gave one. "You can't enter down below. Not yet, son." Then Sampson pushed in the doorbell and a piano elegy responded in eight mournful bars. Footsteps clomped to the door, and a man with a surgical mask pulled down over thick curly hair that ran down to his beard stood at the opened door, letting out a smell of chemicals and something else that made Morris woozy. Along with the noxious odor escaped a heckling laugh, unmistakably female. TV? No. A hiccupy peal that could only come from an open-mouthed woman. Morris stood back at an angle that allowed him to see no farther than the big-armed, squarish man. He wore a rubber apron and his large hands were gloved in thick latex. The man dipped his head, and said, "Sampson" in a baritone. The man, who Morris decided looked part goat and bull, glanced down at the gurney without giving Morris a thought.

"Tall body," the man said of the work that awaited him.

Sampson nodded. "My nephew, Morris. Morris, Omar, our embalmer extraordinaire."

Morris, trying to do what his uncle expected of him, loped forward and extended his hand. The man shook his head no and held up both gloved hands to show they were unclean. The embalmer's stained apron confirmed this.

"Nothing personal," Omar boomed, almost laughing.

Morris shrugged. It made no difference to him. Then he heard the female's laughter, and that caught his attention. Who was she? What was she doing down there?

To satisfy the obvious questions, Sampson said, "Nadira. Our cosmetologist," as if that was enough. Sampson smiled. "Only place to meet her is down below."

Morris felt the need to defend himself and said, "I just didn't think . . ." but then he lost himself and didn't know how else to put it. That a girl would be down there or have anything to laugh about.

With the gurney rolled inside, Sampson had already turned to walk up the ramp. He told his nephew, "Don't you worry. I'm sending you to mortuary school. You'll be down in the thick of things before you know it."

Morris wanted to respond. To speak to the contrary. To represent his own desires, if only he had one. But his words wouldn't come. An inkling rose up within him, but before it gained enough energy for indignation or anger, the piddling inkling flopped.

For the rest of the day, Morris did what Sampson told him. He plugged in the vacuum cleaner with the extra-long cord and ran it up and down the aisle, around the casket area, the viewing path, and the family pew in the main chapel. The Reverence. While the machine growled at the white carpet, he let his mind run with actual thoughts as opposed to simply drifting away. He chased dust and thoughts of her. The girl down below. *What made her laugh? Does she like it down there, with the dead? With the smell? How can she be down there with a part-goat, part-bull-looking man covered in blood?* And again, *What made her laugh?*

He ran the vacuum hard, over and over the same spot. He was glad he couldn't go down below. Glad he never saw the body he'd driven from the morgue. As for mortuary school, he almost laughed, the vacuum's handle throbbing in his grip. He wasn't going to mortuary school. He had no desire to get "down in the thick of things," to touch or look down upon a dead body.

At the end of Morris's first day of work, Sampson told him, "The family will be by tomorrow to make arrangements. I'll show you how to go over their loved one's obituary. You know. Make sure it tells the story of the deceased, however short their story might be."

Morris nodded his yes, although he was certain he didn't want the responsibility.

Sampson gave his nephew a hard thump on the back. It was almost enough to make Morris say, *Yo, Unc. Easy. Take it easy.* He felt those words, but his mouth wouldn't say them. At the end of a day full of firsts and annoyances that had him awake and moving before he was used to, driving when he didn't want to, wheeling a dead body down a narrow ramp, and being poked, slapped, and jabbed from eight to six, he felt steam slowly rising up in him, but then receding.

"Wear a jacket, tie. Nice shirt. Pants. Shoes. No sneakers. And eight o'clock, Morris. Eight. Sharp."

Morris's mother couldn't contain her chattiness when Morris walked into their bungalow house off of Linden Boulevard. "My son, my son, on his first day of real work. Wash up, quick. We're eating."

Morris washed his hands and joined his mother and father at the table. He nodded to his father, who was already enjoying his meal. His father lifted his head and grunted while cutting into his pork loin.

"Well, son." Her smile was hard and expectant. "How was it?"

Morris hated to look at her, for nothing he said

would satisfy her. He'd rather just cut into the meat on his plate. Stab a potato.

He shrugged. But there she sat. Not eating. Waiting on his words. Wanting too much. Finally, he offered, "We picked up a body," hoping that would stop her from asking anything further.

"Who was it?" she asked, almost delighted.

His father dropped his knife and fork. "Woman, you see this good piece of meat I work hard to buy? You think I want to hear this?"

Morris's mother waved her husband off. "Who was it, son? Young? Old? Did he die well, or was he shot up or something horrible like that?"

"For the last time, woman."

Morris didn't know what to do. Talk and make his mother happy. Eat and allow his father to enjoy his meal in peace. Then it occurred to him. His uncle had spared him from viewing the body, so there was no face to recognize. Omar the embalmer wheeled the body "down below," where the smell had made him sick and the woman's laughter pierced him. Even if Morris wanted to make a little mischief at the dinner table, he couldn't. He only knew what he knew of the body. That it was dead. And according to the embalmer, it was tall. About Morris's height.

He stuck a potato in his mouth and chewed. Shrugged.

"What do you mean—?" His mother imitated the shrug, but with a violent jerk. "Of course you know."

He shook his head. Finished swallowing. "No, Mom. I don't. They didn't unzip the bag. I didn't see, so I didn't know." This was the most he had said to his mother, or maybe anyone, at one full clip.

"Well, you should. You should know these things. The people coming in the funeral home. You should pay attention."

Certainly, Mrs. Adler was miffed at Morris for depriving her of a little gossip, but the sight of him dressed in Sunday wear—a suit, shirt, tie, and shoes—in the morning more than made up for last night's disappointment. She was once again holding on to her prayer for Morris. Brimming with hope.

Morris left the house without sitting down to breakfast—he couldn't be late, he said, and was on his way to his uncle's shop. In reality, he meant to make a clean break from his mother. He had heard her stirring around and knew she had been camped at the table. He smelled and wanted the coffee and fried bacon, but his mother wanted to chat, drill, suggest. Encourage him about his future. Truth be told, he was afraid of what would spill out of him if she pushed too hard.

It was an ideal summer morning for the nearly mile walk to the funeral home rather than riding the bus. Even if he dragged along, the route would take him ten minutes. His walk was made uninteresting by the dozen or so blocks of Queens Village homes, elm and linden trees shading each side of Springfield Boulevard. He saw the same rows of bungalows followed by the same rows of aluminum-siding houses all cramped along tight green plots of land.

Finally, a change in the scenery. A half a block ahead, Morris spotted a girl, maybe his age. As he gained on her, he saw she was older by a few years. Girls from school didn't dress like her. Heels, skirt, a fine sweater flung over her back. She was dressed for a job, not to hang out with friends. She carried a leather bag with a handle, the bag the shape and size of a cooler. It was more of a kit than a bag. His eyes left the leather kit in her grip and progressed to the easy sway in her hips.

His legs were longer than hers. He could overtake her in a few steps if he made the effort. Or even approach her. Be near. Smell whatever she sprayed in her hair or on her neck. Or her lotion. Girls rubbed lotion on their legs and arms. As he passed her, he could speak. Say "Morning," like Sampson would. Or "Hey, Miss. Hey, Ms. Hey, sweet . . ." No. He wouldn't say that. He kept walking. Walking was fine. He'd follow as far as she went before he got to the funeral home. And if he caught up to her, then and only then, he'd speak.

But just as he had expected to lose her, she turned and followed the walkway into Eternal Rest Funeral

Home. She swung open the door with no hesitation, like someone at home in Uncle Sampson's shop. And before he knew it, Morris was also marching up the steps behind her, his reflection in the glass door. Surely she had seen him in the glass, but she turned and gave him a smile of surprise.

"Hello," she said.

He cleared his throat to speak. It was her. The girl, or woman, with the laugh. He heard it in the pitch of that one word. "Hello," he managed. Yeah. He got it out and was inwardly proud of his achievement. His pride resulted in a smile, the right response to her broadening, orangey smile.

"Nadira," she said, holding out her free hand.

"Morris." He jumped right on it, holding the door for them and grabbing her hand, but gently. Creamy. He didn't want to crush it, but it was soft. He might even have felt her palm with his thumb in the release.

"Sampson's nephew." She smiled even more. "Welcome. I work down below."

"I know. Down below," he repeated. "Cosmetology."

Orange never looked so welcoming. Succulent. She seemed all right with having been discussed between him and Sampson. "That's right. Hair. Nails. Makeup."

"Do you like it?" he asked.

"Love it," she fired back. "It's for the loved ones."

He couldn't stop himself. Morris kept smiling and

talking. She, Nadira, kept returning fire, and even laughed a bit. She wasn't laughing at him, but with him, when he said, "I guess the fun happens down below." Then she said, "You'll never know until you come on down." And there was another laugh. And Morris was saying to himself, "Down below, down below."

Sampson appeared. "Nadira."

"I know, I know," she said, walking away and winking at Morris. "Around the back. Side door. Down below, where I belong."

Morris watched the cosmetologist, with her leather kit and her heels, walk away.

"It's not a good idea for *them*"—Nadira and Omar, Morris surmised—"to enter through the front, where the clients are. They touch the dead," his uncle said.

"We were just talking."

"Morris."

"Sampson," Morris answered back in the same tone.

"She's got kids," Sampson said. "I'm just giving her a break."

"She's nice," Morris said, fighting the drift. The nod. The silence.

"Did you hear me? Kids."

"I heard," Morris said. "She's nice. Funny." It was so easy to nod. To drift. But he stayed in his voice. In his body. His eyes hurt from fighting the urge to blink. He had never quite done this before. He didn't know why it had been that way, why he had been that way, nor could he remember if he'd always been that way. But at seven minutes or so before eight, something changed.

Sampson's laugh was more of a "humph," then he said, "Don't think your mother'll let her sit at the dinner table."

Morris almost shrugged but caught himself. "We'll see."

"We'll see." Sampson gave another humph.

"We'll see," Morris said, although he couldn't imagine that this woman, cosmetologist, Nadira, would accept an invitation to lunch, let alone to his mother's house for dinner. He smiled. His father might like it.

Sampson shook his head, then shoved a typed page at his nephew. "Here's the deceased's obituary. The mother was too distraught to deal with it, so his sister wrote it. Young girl. But she did it." He nodded toward the office. "Sit down. Look it over. Make sure it's, you know, spelled correctly. Tells the story."

The sister had used a big font, just like he used to when he ran out of sentences to fill essay paragraphs. Her brother, in his nineteen years, had accomplished more than Morris had, but that came as no surprise. Morris, at eighteen, had just had his first real conversation with a female other than his mother. The girl's dead brother had graduated from high school—Morris's high school, in fact. He ran cross-country. Did one year of York Community College and had held a few part-time jobs.

Morris read the sheet again, not knowing what he was looking for, besides misspelled words: a *there* instead of a *their*, a plural verb that should be singular. He certainly didn't feel he was the right one to correct the grieving girl's account of her brother's life. As short as the obituary was, it made the deceased a guy. Real. Male and a brother. Loved by a mother and grandmother. Missed by the cross-country team.

He placed the obituary on his uncle's desk. Nodded and said, "It's fine."

The family arrived at seven minutes after nine.

"I'm sorry for your loss," Morris said to the tall woman in the middle. A woman near his mother's age. The mother of the deceased. She was accompanied by an older woman who resembled her but had an ashen face and was stooped over. The grandmother of the deceased. And there was the sister. His age. No. A year or two younger.

The older woman, who had been supported by her granddaughter, grabbed his arm. Her fingers were long and formed quite the grip. Morris led the family slowly down the carpeted hall and into the office. The chairs had already been arranged for their visit. Sampson rose and greeted the family once they entered the office, while Morris awkwardly helped the grandmother into her chair. Only then did she release his arm. Morris wanted to rub the feeling back into his arm but didn't. Besides, he felt the girl staring, perhaps waiting to see if he would.

When he took his place in the corner nearest Sampson, as his uncle had instructed him, he noticed that the deceased's sister's eyes were still fixed on him. He didn't know where to look, but wherever he turned, he felt her.

Sampson had their file on his desk. The deceased's name, last, then first, printed neatly on the folder's tab. Morris fought to remain alert, interested, while Sampson guided the mother of the deceased through the details of casket choice, funeral cars, programs, prayer cards, and fan selections. July. The height of summer. Fans were a must. Morris was mildly surprised that his uncle could be gentle. He admired the delicate way Sampson went about inquiring into the insurance policy and the "final place of repose."

Through it all, the sister's eyes never left Morris. So Morris did what he never would have done before. He refused to drift away. He was determined to stay. Fill himself with himself. Instead of looking off somewhere safe, Morris returned the girl's stare. But she was better at it.

A little more than an hour earlier, he had had his first real conversation with a girl. A woman. Now he was the staring target of a dead guy's sister. If her stare was like a sophomore girl's gaze at a senior, he'd be flushed with a good discomfort that said, *Today is a good day. Today Morris Adler entered his life.* But her stare was hardly a gaze.

Eventually he backed down and looked again at the folder on the desk with the tab sticking out and the deceased's name written in black felt-tip in Sampson's heavy-handed slant. Then he looked back up at her. Her eyes. Her face.

And now he knew whose body he had collected, driven, and rolled down the ramp that led to the workroom down below. How could he not know? He'd seen that face, more or less, on a much taller guy. Yes. He knew the deceased. Or knew *of* the deceased. The brother. So, in a way, he knew the sister without actually knowing her.

When the sister was certain of this, she gave him a small nod while Sampson and the mother continued making arrangements. She nodded again.

Across from her, there sat Morris Adler, staring into open eyes that made up for the ones that were closed, down below. He didn't have to see her brother's face or read the obituary to know who he was. Even if he could drift away, there was no point. What else could he do? He nodded to her. A small nod between them.

INITIATION

ELLEN HOPKINS

MICK GALINDO sat on the porch swing, clipping his toenails. As porches went, his (okay, Mama's) was rather narrow, with sagging steps and weathered posts and rafters that creaked beneath his weight. That didn't much worry him, though. His mother, who topped the scales at close to three hundred, had rocked in this swing without incident for years. Mick doubted his hundred sixty-eight pounds would bring it crashing down.

It was late July, and anywhere else it would be hellhole hot. The whispers of a breeze managed to cool the late afternoon just enough to make it bearable. Inside the house, Mama hovered in front of a big fan, attempting "Ave Maria." Her low notes reverberated pleasantly enough, but when she reached too high, the sound was very much like a screech owl. In pain. Probably half the reason Papa took off when Mick was eleven.

The years without him were, at once, better and worse. Better because though he had kept Papa's Latino surname, Mick was almost as fair as Mama, and most people assumed he was of Italian descent. Worse because Mama was forced to work, too hard for a woman of her age and bulk, as a housekeeper and nanny for a moneyed penthouse dweller in the city. Her mood, already sour with Papa's desertion, grew testier with every forced smile and phony "Happy to, sir."

"Miguel!" Mama called. "Come in here."

"No soy Miguel, Mama. Me llamo Mick." He wasn't Miguel, the Spanish equivalent of Michael. His name was Mick. He liked that better. It reflected Mama's heritage. She was Irish, so why did she insist on sounding south-of-the-border? Then again, he had just answered her *en español.* Too much of Papa remained.

He went inside, blinking away sun glare. "What is it, Mama?"

She sprawled in her lopsided easy chair, the guts of the Sunday *Daily News* surrounding her. "Did you see this? Did you know him?" She jabbed at the obituary page. "Right there." She tapped. "Kevin."

Nicholas, Kevin. Age 19. Died at York Hospital, July 19, 2012.

There was a lot more. "Survived bys" and the few highlights of Kevin's few years. Graduated high school with honors. Captain of the cross-country team. Majored in business at York Community College. Part-time jobs at Starbucks and the campus bookstore. Wow. They made the guy sound squeaky clean. If they only knew.

Still, he was way too young to die.

There but for the grace of God . . . Mick swayed slightly. "No, Mama. I hadn't heard."

"But you knew the boy, didn't you?" Expectation glimmered in her heavy-lidded eyes.

"Yes, Mama. We were . . . friends."

Truth be told, he hadn't seen Kevin in a while. The cross-country-star business major had not exactly been happy about Mick taking an interest in his little sister. Junior or no, Lydia was incredible, with the face of an angel, haloed in a shine of black hair, and eyes like a storm-shadowed sea. An ocean you would drown in happily. It had probably been in poor taste to admit how often he'd thought about seeing her naked. "Touch my sister, and I'll show you the way to hell" were the last words Mick would ever hear from Kevin now.

But when they were kids, oh yes, he and Kev had been tight. It had started with altar-boy duty. Mick's parents had agreed on one thing—raising their son as a strict Catholic. If he had a dollar for every Hail Mary he'd been forced to repeat, he'd be living on Park Avenue. After they'd left the stench of the landfill behind, the first thing Katherine Galindo had done was to pay a call on the local priest.

Father Holbrook was not an imposing man of God by any means. In fact, he was elf-like—miniature in height and frail as a wooden matchstick. Mick, a slender ten-year-old, could have taken him at arm wrestling. Except, of course, Mama would have had none of that.

She'd introduced him like this: "Meet my son, Michael." Not Miguel. Father Holbrook's parish was .27 percent Hispanic. "He's a good Catholic. Perhaps a priest one day. Meanwhile, he wants to become an altar boy. Next year, when he's old enough to learn the requirements."

At that point in his life, Mick had considered himself a fair enough Catholic. He enjoyed Mass, and when he went forward to celebrate Communion, the presence of God came over him, brought comfort. He prayed diligently to Jesus and Mother Mary, was semifaithful to the rosary. But it had not crossed his mind that he wanted to be an altar boy. That was Mama's dream. Regardless, it was one he was destined to fulfill. Fate, he decided, was synonymous with his mother's desires.

The year that followed was difficult. Papa found work on a fishing boat. It paid well enough, but he hated "spending every day kneeling in slime and groping guts." All to please his wife, who wanted "the finer things in life." Their neighbors were either stuffy or nosy, and neither type suited Mama, who grew grumpier, it seemed, by the day. This led to frequent arguments with Papa. And when they weren't fighting, they didn't speak at all.

Mick started fifth grade in a school where he knew no one. As a dedicated introvert, he wasn't exactly a friend magnet and spent his after-school hours with his nose in a book. Words! The bigger, the better. Those he didn't know, he looked up. He absorbed them like mashed potatoes mopping up gravy. They gave him power, fueled his imagination, made him smarter than your average Joe (not Jose). Not that anyone noticed.

Mama was too busy being miserable. Despondent. Melancholy. Mick liked that word especially. Reminded him of cauliflower, his favorite vegetable, at least when it was smothered in cheese.

Papa mostly cared about the World Cup. "Why don't you play soccer?" he asked one day, midmatch and midsix-pack. "You're not a little girl, are you?"

Never mind that on the local youth soccer team, girls played right along with the boys. "No, Papa. It's just . . . I'm not . . . interested in sports."

Papa clucked his tongue. "Every boy worth a decent boner likes sports. Get your ass over here."

Reluctantly, Mick joined his father on the thirdhand sofa. Papa offered him a sip of Pabst, but Mick shook his head. "Smells like pee."

Papa laughed. Guffawed. Then he reconsidered. "You *like* girls, don't you?"

Mick didn't particularly like anyone, female or male. But that wasn't the answer Papa wanted. "Sure, I like girls."

"Especially girls like those, no?" Papa pointed to the TV, where two women with giant chests, made obvious with too-tight tank tops, talked up their favorite players.

Mick knew what Papa wanted him to say. "Mmm. Nice breasts."

"You mean tits. Scrumptious tits."

"Oh, yeah."

Color commentary over, the fuzzy station rejoined the game. Mick suffered the next two Pabst/pee-perfumed hours cheering or sighing, on Papa's cue. But he hadn't joined the soccer team that year, or any other.

That summer, Mick began his altar-attendant training. There wasn't much to learn, really. When to ring the bell. How to swing the cloying incense so it wouldn't overwhelm the presiding priest. Father Holbrook introduced the kids who would participate in the biweekly lessons: "William Benedict. Michael Galindo. Candace Lomack. Kevin Nicholas."

Mick knew Will from school—he was another quiet loner, which is probably why Mick had noticed him. Candy and Kevin were older, so went to middle school. Kevin's charisma was magnetic, and he immediately claimed the role of leader. He was tall, with the same dark eyes as his sister and a feral smile that concealed the angry energy he harbored inside. That he smiled at Mick at all seemed a surprising invitation to kinship. By then, Mick hungered for a friend.

"Where you from?" was how Kevin broke the ice.

"Swedesboro. Jersey. Left 'cause of the landfill. You know, the smell." Why'd he say that? *You know, the smell.*

Kevin let it go. "You gotta lose the accent. These hoity-toities around here think they're better than Jersey."

Of course. The accent. Without it, maybe he'd assimilate better. "Thanks. I'll work on it."

"There's something else there, too. Galindo, right?"

Mick's face flushed. "Yeah." Jersey all the way. But did Papa also leak through?

"That's cool. But try for Yankee."

For whatever reason, Kevin took Mick under his wing. He showed him the best pizza spots. The best places to skate in the park. Whose backyards to avoid cutting through and, if anybody called the cops, which uniforms you could talk to and which you should run from. They even discussed the possibility of becoming

25

priests one day. By summer's end, Mick started to feel assimilated.

The outside activity came with an added benefit: he could escape his parents' relentless bickering. It was a tide, lapping at the foundation of their marriage. At some level, Mick knew the wall was doomed to disintegrate. What he didn't realize was how soon.

In the fall, Mick moved to the middle school, and there he had a solid ally in Kevin Nicholas. This bolstered both his courage and his ego. Though he wasn't exactly sixth-grade top dog, he made his way into the midlevel pack. And that rocked.

On Saturdays, Mick hung out with Kevin, skating and looking for hot girls. Mick wasn't exactly sure what *hot* meant. It had something to do with breasts, right? Or tits? Maybe they weren't all sticking out of bikini tops, but you could tell they were there. Anyway, what did it matter? It wasn't like he and Kev were going to hook up with hot girls, or any girls. Still, he didn't want Kevin to think he was a total dork. "You know who's kind of hot? Candy Lomack."

"The altar girl? I guess I never noticed."

Mick insisted, "Well, she is. She's got awesome tits." He wasn't exactly sure that was so, because she kept them pretty well covered. What he did know was, unlike some other girls her age, she definitely had them.

"I'll check 'em out tomorrow at Mass." Game on.

It was an interesting Sunday. Both Mick and Kevin spent way too much time trying to assess the state of Candy's boobs, a hard thing to do when they were well disguised beneath vestments. The altar service suffered as a result. Only Candy, who was somehow unaware of the boys' gazes, managed to do the right thing at the right time. Father Holbrook was livid.

"May I see you two for a few minutes?" he asked once the church cleared.

They followed him to his office. Waited as he took a big key ring from his desk drawer, unlocked the sacristy door, and de-robed.

"Hope he's got something on under there," Kevin whispered. "Last thing I ever want to see is Father H naked."

"Totally!" agreed Mick, stifling a laugh. Just barely.

Father Holbrook returned, fully clothed, relocked the sacristy, and put the keys back in his desk drawer before saying, "Your inattention today was not appreciated, and I saw where your eyes kept wandering. Don't neglect confession this week."

They didn't. But no amount of penance could keep Kevin from hatching a plan to see Candy's tits totally uncovered. It was a brilliant plot, really, except for one major detail, and it might not have gone down at all. But then Papa went away. Came home midday. Showered off the fish guts. Packed a few clean clothes. Left a note as his good-bye: *Going back to Jersey. I prefer my air dirty. My women, too.*

Anger, hurt, and a smidgeon of guilt (what if he'd decided to play soccer?) weighted Mick. He carried that burden in the clench of his jaw, the slack of his shoulders. It went with him everywhere—school, beach, church. Candy noticed it there during eight a.m. Mass. Afterward, she said, "I heard your dad left. That must be really hard. Do you want to talk about it?"

Her voice was maple syrup, her eyes the blue of summer-lush hydrangea. And yes, beneath her tight angora sweater, there were mounds. Breasts. Maybe even tits. He was moved, but with something much more primitive than love. And then it struck him. Perhaps that major detail had just resolved itself. "Yes," he said. "I would really appreciate talking about it. You don't have to be home right away, do you?"

Candy shook her head. "My parents are out of town. I'm staying with my grandma. She won't care if I'm late." Providence.

Mick went to find Kevin. "Candy wants to talk. I think the cemetery might be a good place. Can you handle the rest?"

Kev's eyes lit up. "As soon as the ten o'clock begins. No-brainer. I'll meet you there."

It was 9:43. Mick went back to Candy. "Let's take a walk."

People crowded the front doors, so Mick took her hand and pulled her toward the side exit. He had never touched a girl before. Well, not like this. Not with deviltry in mind. They stepped into the autumn morning, and Mick inhaled a deep breath of air, scented heavily with burning leaves. "Smells like death."

"What do you mean?"

"The death of a season. Soon, another year. Come on."

He led the way toward the back of the church and across the parking lot, which was full of cars but emptied of people. Into the tangled woods, whose branches were only beginning to drop their burdens. Fall light dappled through a curtain of tangerine and auburn. The leaf mosaic shimmered overhead.

"Where are we going?"

"Up here." Almost immediately, they broke out of the trees. Before them was a huge expanse of fading grass studded with headstones. He glanced at his watch: nine fifty-five. "Do you have anyone buried here?"

"You mean, like someone I know?"

"Yeah."

"Uh-uh. My parents are from Massachusetts. All our relatives are buried there. At least, I think so."

Mick started across the graves. "Kevin says these

people must have been losers. They didn't have any loved ones who wanted to be buried next to them, so they got planted out here all alone."

"That's sad." She stopped to study one gravestone. Hesitated before cutting between it and the adjoining slab. "But how would Kevin know?"

Mick kept moving forward, across a dirt tract and onto a large section of graves, very close together. "He's been here a lot, I guess. His dad is right over there."

"Oh, wow." Engaged, she trailed him to another periphery, shaded by stubborn oaks.

"There." Mick pointed to a low marble mound. The simple engraving read:

LAWRENCE NICHOLAS

1968–2004

BELOVED HUSBAND AND FATHER

A thin thread of music drifted up from the church, through the woods and across the cemetery. The ten o'clock Mass had begun. How long would it take Kevin to sneak into Father Holbrook's office, take the keys from his desk, open the sacristy, and find the store of altar wine?

Other than little sips at Communion and a couple of stolen tastes from Mama's glasses, Mick had never imbibed. How much would it take to get drunk? And could they talk Candy into getting drunk, too?

Suddenly, he was aware of her asking him something. "Sorry. What?"

"I said, how did Kevin's father die? He wasn't even forty."

Mick shrugged. "You can ask Kevin about it. He'll be here in a minute."

The bridge of Candy's nose disappeared into a pair of deep frown lines. If she kept that up, she was going to get early wrinkles. "Why is Kevin coming?"

Mick grinned. "It's a surprise." He sat on a patch of grass between two graves, patted the ground beside him.

Candy sat very close beside him. So close that he could smell her hair, which wore some tropical perfume. Nice. Really nice. "What about your dad? Do you miss him?"

Mick shrugged, and the smile fell away from his face. "At least he isn't dead. I don't think so, anyway. We haven't heard a word from him since he left."

Suddenly, Kevin burst through the brush and came sprinting across the lawn. He was laughing, and his abdomen bulged suspiciously. When he reached them, he plopped straight down on his father's grave. "Hey, Dad," he said. "Great to see you!" Then he reached up under his shirt and whipped out a full bottle of sherry. "Let's drink to the son of a bitch!"

Candy gasped. "Where did you get that?"

God, Mick thought, *she isn't going to get pissy, is she?*

But then Kevin said, "Father H donated it. He thought it was getting a little old."

Candy laughed and reached for the bottle. "Let me taste it. I wouldn't want you to get sick or something." Mick and Kevin exchanged a long look as Candy unscrewed the bottle and tipped it into her mouth. Then she handed it back to Kevin. "Think it's okay."

And off they went, passing that syrupy wine among them like three old winos in a backstreet alley. Mick noticed a weird little buzz in his ears before the bottle was half-gone. "What's that noise? Cicadas?"

Kevin snorted. "The cicadas died weeks ago. Jeez. Are you getting fuzzy already?"

"I am," said Candy before taking another long pull. "Feels great."

"Wow," said Kevin. "I had no idea you were that kind of a girl. Have you done this before?"

She drew those startling blue eyes level with his. "Last summer. At camp. A couple of the counselors swiped some and shared it with a few of us girls."

"Why would they do that?" asked Mick. He was pretty sure he already knew the answer. But somehow he just couldn't find it.

"Well, why do you think?" Her hand settled on his thigh. It was warm. And it moved.

Holy moly! No. Holy crap! Would he actually get to

see her tits? Something just south of his belly button, and very near her fingers, writhed.

But then she withdrew her hand. Took another sip before offering the bottle to Kevin. "How did your dad die?" Her honey voice had grown noticeably thicker.

"Bastard blew his brains out." He let that sink in before adding, "Guess who found him?"

Candy gulped. "You? That's awful!" She reached out to touch his cheek.

Kevin threw his arm up, blocking the gesture. It was the first glimpse Mick ever got of the serpent living inside his friend. But as quickly as it surfaced, it vanished again. "Sorry. Didn't mean that. Not your fault. Sometimes . . . when I think about it . . . I get pissed."

"It's okay. I'm sorry, too." Candy's voice echoed into the bottle, which kept getting emptier.

The buzz in Mick's ears had moved inside his head. Swallowed his brain. Did the others feel that way, too? They must. So this was what it meant to get drunk. He liked it. Sort of. All manner of bad stuff faded away. The dizzy part, he didn't care for so much.

And then it happened. "Do you believe in ghosts?" asked Kevin.

Mick shook his head as Candy said, "No. Why?"

"I think I've been possessed." The snake surfaced

again. "You have to be my exorcist," he said to Candy. "And there's only one way to do it."

"How?" she asked, but her seductive smile said she knew exactly what he was after.

Kevin reached over and started working her buttons. When he fumbled, she actually helped him! It couldn't be that easy. But inch by inch, more skin was exposed until the blouse peeled totally away. Mick couldn't help but stare. He'd never seen anything so . . . real. Now his head was really spinning.

That altar girl may have been only thirteen, but she had the tits of a woman. And she knew things that women did, too, like how to use her hands to make a boy feel really good. Two boys, in fact. It was the first, and so maybe the best, sex he'd ever had. And he'd fifty-fiftied it with Kevin. Later, his stomach churned sticky, sweet bile and his head felt like someone had hammered a chisel through it. Kev didn't fare much better. But the boys agreed on four things.

One: An altar girl did not a saint make.

Two: Alcohol plus a good sob story equaled sex.

Three: Some things were worth a hangover.

Four: They were not cut out to be priests.

That wasn't the only illicit thing they shared over the next few years. But then Mick went crazy over Lydia. Some things a brother can't offer a friend, not even a best friend.

Suddenly, Mick realized he could call her now. She would need consoling.

"When is the funeral?" he asked Mama. "We should offer our condolences."

Maybe he should even stand up and speak. Mick smiled at a sudden slice of inspiration.

Perhaps the graveyard story would make a good eulogy.

JUST ONCE

A.S. KING

CANDY LOMACK GROANED and rolled over. It was too early. For anything. Especially for what Tyler was suggesting.

"Come on. Just once?"

She groaned again and moved farther away from him, indicating a no. So he did it himself and she pretended she was asleep.

Hadn't her life been a series of *Just Onces*?

Starting with summer camp when she was twelve . . . and what those counselors did with her. Come on, Candy, just drink it once? Just kiss me once? Just touch it once? Just try it once?

Tyler rolled out of bed and into his clothes and left through the window, the way he'd come in the night before. She didn't even like him. She was executing some kind of self-dare. He was the guy everyone was afraid of. *Out of control. Too much. Too dangerous.* This was her habit—self-dares and dating boys who would scare most practical girls into a coma. Most of them really weren't that scary and just acted it. Damaged goods. Inside they were just people like everyone else. Candy knew plenty about damaged goods.

She rolled back over and faced the empty half of the bed where Tyler had just been. She took the top sheet and rolled it into a ball with her feet and pushed it to the floor. She grabbed a nearby black T-shirt and slipped it over her head and reached for her laptop. As it powered up, she propped herself on pillows and stretched and looked at the clock. It was 11:07. Entirely too early to be up on a hot July morning after a long night of serving drinks . . . and drinking drinks.

First stop: e-mail. Spam and more spam. *Want to go all night long? Best diet weight-loss pill! NOTICE OF YOUR FUNDS £100 MILLION! Satisfactory sexual intercourse!*

"Satisfactory sexual intercourse." Candy laughed. *Sounds like something a second grade teacher would say.*

An e-mail from her mother. Mrs. Regina Lomack. The woman who lived beyond Candy's bedroom door and communicated with Candy mostly through e-mails now. The woman who named her Candy—a tag that would follow her through life and make her as attractive to men as candy on the grass is attractive to ants. The woman who wouldn't let her move out but wouldn't let her live there, either.

At eighteen years old, Candy Lomack was in limbo. Not here, but here. Not working but working. Not earning but earning just enough to get by. Not living but living enough to have a guy like Tyler mess up her sheets in the morning.

At eighteen years old, Candy Lomack was still using her window as a door and parking on the side road next to the park to avoid seeing her parents.

She deleted her mother's e-mail without reading it.

Next stop: Facebook.

First, a barrage of requests from her high-school friend Jane to play some stupid games. Hidden Gems and Farmerville and Pirate's Booty. *Who has time for these games?* Candy thought. Jane was more than three years older than her, but completely immature. Never partied or got with boys. Never even came home late once. Jane was boring.

But she had a perfect life now, fresh out of college with two degrees—a BA in teaching and an MRS. Candy had gone to the wedding. It was boring. Jane had a house up in Connecticut and would start her first teaching job in the fall. Second grade. *Satisfactory sexual intercourse,* Candy thought. That's what Jane probably had. And Candy had Tyler.

As she scrolled through posts on Facebook, she found

two old boyfriends from middle school who posted completely opposite political status updates and then simultaneously argued on each other's posts. Candy remembered when those boys had lives beyond the pointless world of politics. *Really. Who gives a shit? Nothing ever changes.*

Then she saw the post from Lydia. She was never sure why she had accepted Lydia's friend request, but she had. Lydia hadn't ever done anything bad to her. She was a good kid. Younger than Candy.

The post said: *R.I.P. to my brother Kevin. We'll miss you.*

Candy scanned the comment trail. *We're thinking of you. We're praying for you and your family. So sorry to hear of Kevin's passing. Let us know if there's anything we can do.* This wasn't a joke.

She reread it. *R.I.P. to my brother Kevin. We'll miss you.*

And it sank in.

Kevin Nicholas was dead.

Candy stared at the words on the screen. And then she laughed. Not loudly. But it rose from her like vomit — unintended and foul smelling. Her stomach heaved with how funny it was. She had to sit up and catch her breath. Then it started again, and she laughed until she cried, and as she wiped the tears away, she was sure they were happy tears.

How many times had she said, "Just go to hell, Kevin!"

R.I.P. Kevin Nicholas, my ass. Rest in hell. Rest in

all the shit you gave me. Rest never. Hope you die soon. Again. Selfish bastard.

She retrieved the e-mail from her mother from the trash folder. Indeed, it was this news: *I thought you should know Kevin Nicholas died. It was in the paper today. I'm going to send flowers from the family, so you don't need to worry about that.*

In the next paragraph, sitting on its own like a lonely girl at recess, was this line: *If you want to talk, I'm here.*

"Just what I need," Candy said aloud. "You. Here."

She flopped out of bed, placed the closed laptop on her bureau, and walked straight into the shower, where it really hit her.

Kevin Nicholas is dead.

Kevin fucking Nicholas.

The first boy I fell in love with.

The boy who showed me that maybe I was worth loving.

The boy I gave my whole self to.

The boy who never gave himself to me.

The boy who stopped talking. Stopped holding hands. Stopped smiling. Damaged goods.

Dead.

The shower water made it pointless to wipe the tears away. But even Candy knew that this time these weren't happy tears. These were the saddest tears she'd cried since the day he'd broken up with her when she was fourteen over by the CVS on Springfield. She remembered that now, in the shower. How she'd watched all the people in the parking lot doing normal things while she'd sat holding her aching guts. How she'd walked the rest of the way home without him, claiming she'd rather be dead or kidnapped or whatever happened to girls walking alone on the roads than be without Kevin.

As it turned out, she got home.

And there stood Mrs. Regina Lomack, who was looking at her in that way she did, with her hands on her hips and a smile on her face. When Candy saw the smile, she wanted to smack it right off. Instead she gave her mother a chance to talk. Maybe something good had happened to them. Maybe Dad had finally gotten another job and they could leave Queens and move somewhere interesting.

"It this yours?" Regina had asked, pulling a used pregnancy test from behind her back and holding it in front of her the way a crossing guard might use a sign to help little children walk to school.

"Yes," Candy had answered. "But I'm not pregnant." She wasn't sure why she added it. It seemed to anger her mother more. But in the grand scheme of things, that was good news, right?

"I don't know what to say anymore," Mrs. Lomack said. "So I've made an appointment with Father

Holbrook. Maybe he can talk sense into your head. Come on. We're going now." Mrs. Lomack put the used pregnancy test into her purse.

"You're taking it with you?"

"What?"

"That!" Candy pointed to the test.

"Well, how else do I tell him?"

Candy got into her mother's car for the drive to church, less than five minutes away. She sat in the backseat to make it seem like what it really was. And in the emptiness of that backseat, it hit her that Kevin had just broken up with her. She remembered every time she'd said "I love you" and every time he'd said it back. Every time he'd squeezed her hand like he really did love her. They were soul mates, she'd thought. *Meant to be.* Kevin, though often stuck inside himself, could *talk* to Candy. Except when he didn't. Except when he talked to other girls instead. Remembering this, she started to cry the tears she hadn't been able to cry outside the CVS on Springfield. The tears she couldn't let Kevin see because he'd just yell at her, which is what he always did when she cried.

Stop trying to control me by crying. You piss me off so much when you do that!

Kevin's father used to cry. At dinner. At baseball games. At church. At TV shows that weren't even sad. Mr. Nicholas—dead at thirty-six—had what Regina

Lomack called "issues," which was all she ever said, even though she'd known him for years through church.

Mr. Nicholas's issues had led him to put a gun in his mouth and pull the trigger. Kevin talked about it sometimes. The first time was right after the day in the cemetery with that bottle of sherry, him, and Mick from New Jersey.

She'd said, "If you ever want to talk to me about that, you know you can, right?"

"I found him, you know? It was the grossest thing I ever saw," he'd said, and then he'd looked at her for a long time. The look in his eyes had nothing to do with talking anymore. So they started to date. Talking happened occasionally. Kissing happened more often. Other things happened in between. During cross-country races, she'd cheer him on and bring him water and a towel when he was done. By Christmas, he'd *just-onced* his way into touching her in places she'd never been touched before. Then, by Easter, when the vestments in the church were purple and the mood was joyous after a hard winter, he *just-onced* his way into *it*. Doing the real *it*. And afterward, as they lay in Candy's double bed while her parents were at work, Kevin described what he'd seen.

"He didn't have a head anymore, you know?" he said. "All that was left was a jaw and one of his ears. And it was all exploded and big even though there wasn't much of anything there." Anyone else saying this would have cried, but not Kevin. He looked straight at the ceiling and told it like he'd tell a dirty joke or give a guy with out-of-state plates directions to the nearest restaurant.

"What'd you do?" she'd asked.

"I called the cops. What the fuck else would I do?"

"Sorry," she'd said.

"You're such a dipshit sometimes, Candy."

She hadn't said it, but she'd thought it: *So you just fucked a dipshit, then.*

Every time they did it after that—up until the day outside the CVS—Kevin would turn on her like that. From lamb to lion. No warning, no trigger that she could see. Maybe something inside his head felt happy, so he had to go and ruin it. That's what she concluded anyway, after nearly nine months of dating. If that's what you'd call all those nights she sat waiting for him to talk to her or call her or touch her or say *I love you* after another *just once.* Dating, sure. More like blowing time.

The pregnancy test was five days old when her mother found it. Candy had hidden it in the garage trash can, so her mother had to have been on some sort of mission in order to find it. As they drove, Regina Lomack ignored her daughter's crying in the backseat. Only when they stepped into Father Holbrook's office did Regina eventually find out what she was upset about.

Regina placed the pregnancy test, partially wrapped in a tissue, on the priest's desk.

"Ew. I peed on that," Candy protested. She snatched it from the desk and put it on the chair next to her leg.

"Candace, I don't understand," Father Holbrook started. "When you came to me and started lessons, you and I discussed how girls should act. I know you've been seeing Kevin Nicholas, and I hoped it was a friendship more than anything. Especially at your age." He trailed off into thought. "I think our first step is to break it off between the two of you. It's clearly not a healthy relationship if you've already begun doing things like this."

"I hate God," Candy said. Out of nowhere. She wasn't even sure if it was true. So she said it again. "There is no God."

Regina Lomack slapped her then. Father Holbrook leaned forward.

Candy continued. "And you don't have to worry. Kevin broke up with me today. He found another girlfriend."

She started to sob then, rehearing everything Kevin had said to her in front of the CVS: "*You're just always pissing me off, you know? Always talking. Great tits aren't everything. Anyway, Laura has birth-control pills, and I can't handle another week like last week. Jesus. How could you be so stupid to almost get pregnant? Everyone knows about that shit.*"

45

She didn't *know* about that shit. All Candy was ever taught in school was how to not have sex. Abstinence education, they called it. Which was, as it turned out, no education at all—just the lack of it.

"Good," Father Holbrook said. "I'm glad you're away from him. He's trouble. It's not my place to say it, but I think the boy needs counseling after what he's already seen in his life." Then he looked at Mrs. Lomack and said, "Regina, I think Candace needs to spend more time here. If she says she hates God, we need to make her understand that God isn't the problem."

"Agreed," said Mrs. Lomack.

He looked back at Candy. "You'll go to confession and get this sorted out. Then you'll meet me here every Monday, Wednesday, and Friday to clean."

"To clean?"

"It's time you learned your place in the world. Maybe more time in the church will remind you why you want to stay away from trouble."

"Agreed," Mrs. Lomack repeated.

"You get one chance at life, Candace. It's a glorious and amazing gift. I'll see you here at eight a.m. tomorrow."

Regina grabbed her arm then and the pregnancy test dropped onto the floor and Candy went to pick it up, but Father Holbrook said, "Leave it."

The drive home was quiet. They took Hempstead Ave., and it was crowded on a Sunday. Candy sat in the backseat again and stared out the window. She couldn't believe it — the day had been so surreal. First Kevin, and then her mother and the used pregnancy test and Father Holbrook. The whole week had been unreal. Starting with telling Kevin about maybe being pregnant, to buying the pregnancy test at CVS with Kevin after telling him, to him being moody instead of happy when the line turned out to be a minus instead of a plus. She was so happy that it didn't occur to her that he wouldn't be, too. But it should have occurred to her after nearly nine months of being Kevin's girlfriend.

There was medication now for what Kevin had. For what his father had. Something to even out the ups and downs and make life less intense. She talked about it a few times with him, always getting the same answer. The Nicholases didn't believe in that sort of thing, he'd said.

"God cures all," he said. "If you believe my mother."

And killing yourself cures all . . . if I believe your father.

Four years later and Kevin Nicholas was dead. Candy still lived at home even though she had a full-time job at the local brewing company, serving food and beer. She didn't go to church anymore. Not after the three months of cleaning toilets and floors and not after acting out penance upon penance at the altar and not after the *just once* of Sister Helen, who had taken her under her wing during the summer of atonement.

She had stopped going by simply disappearing. It became a game. Her parents would lock up her windows, so she'd sneak out the door. They got deadbolt locks and hid the key, and she'd squeeze out through the bathroom window. They locked that, and so she took to not coming home on Saturday nights at all.

Sometimes as she roamed the roads late on Saturday nights, she'd seen Kevin and his new girl, Laura. Smoking joints. Drinking cans of beer behind the shopping center. Then school started up again, and Kevin moved on to other girls. She saw him once in their old spot in the park, two figures on the grass with Kevin's plaid blanket beneath them. She tried to look away, but she couldn't. She watched until they were done.

Then she looked at her phone and noted the time: 11:46. By 11:58 he was climbing the rocks by himself and whatever poor girl he'd just *just onced* sat staring into space, holding her knees and rocking. Probably trying to figure out the puzzle because she didn't know yet that there were pieces missing. *Probably wondering if he meant it when he said she was beautiful,* Candy thought. *He never meant it. To Kevin nothing was beautiful.*

She'd tried to stay friends with him. First love and all that. You stay friends. You help when he's down. You pray some nights that he stops hanging around with the wrong guys. White and angry with no reason. Stuck on Hollis Ave. and listening to rap music with the bass so high you can hear them coming. You pray, but nothing happens—which is proof that she was right when she said it. *There is no God.*

They made a crew. Not like any of the real gangs you see on TV, but maybe the same kind of mentality. And Kev was the perfect draw. Running star. Senior. Good-looking. Got the girls and knew what to do with them. Even Mick had joined in for a while until things started to get too heavy. She wasn't sure what Mick meant when he'd said it to her. What could those boys do in this little place that would be so dangerous? So she asked, and Mick said, "Initiations."

Which made it no less of a mystery.

A year after they'd broken up and Candy had moved on to the next dare—a kid named Tom who was in foster care—Kevin's little sister, Lydia, approached her in school. She said, "I know you still love him, but I'm telling you, girl. You're better off. He's not right. We don't know what to do."

"He won't talk to me anymore," Candy offered. "Not since the crew."

"The crew is so stupid," Lydia said.

"Mick got out," Candy said. "I hear he likes you."

Lydia looked down at the newly shined public-school

linoleum. "Not my type," she said. "Anyway, he's Kev's best friend. Kev would kill us both if he ever found out. Like *Scarface,* you know?"

Candy had never seen *Scarface,* but she nodded.

That year Kevin graduated and tried to get himself together. Went to college a little. But he was still on the roller coaster. She could see it in the slumped way he walked sometimes. How simultaneously overconfident he was. How the two Kevins fit into one body. She could see it and she was sorry for his whole life. He didn't deserve it—what had happened to him. It wasn't fair that he was on a crusade to kill his own happiness. But things happen.

Shit happens.

The last time she saw him, she served him at the brewery. It was about a month ago. He brought in some friends from college and held court. He was nice, but every time she walked away from the table, the boys laughed and she knew he was talking about her.

She smoked a joint outside the kitchen door with Caesar, the blue-eyed waiter.

"That table of assholes giving you a hard time?" he asked.

"Nah. I know them," she said. "Or one of them, anyway." *I guess.*

■ ■ ■

When she stepped out of the shower, she toweled off and opened her computer again. Four more Facebook condolences. She tried to add one to make it five, but she couldn't think of anything to say. This wasn't a throwaway thing, Kevin Nicholas. He wasn't an ordinary boy who just happened to die. He was damaged goods. Her first love. He was something special, even though he never saw it. He deserved something more than a stupid Facebook post. He deserved more than some inoffensive flowers her mother would send. He deserved a life. And who doesn't make mistakes? Just once? Everyone makes mistakes. Just once.

THE NEXT NEXT LEVEL

TORREY MALDONADO

"KEVIN'S DEAD," my dad said, slowly easing into the seat across from me at our dining-room table. "His mother just texted and asked me to tell you. She said he . . ."

I stared up from my cell and watched my dad's hand set his BlackBerry facedown. My eyes went to his lips. Words came out of his mouth but my mind hit mute on the rest of what he said.

I didn't go deaf on him because I was still tight from our earlier argument and wished he'd poof into a cloud of smoke and disappear.

And I wasn't tuning him out because of the earbud in my right ear blasting this sick beat over and over.

He and everything in front of me just instantly went TV-screen-blip-black off because the words "Kevin's dead" just couldn't compute. They short-circuited my whole everything.

How could Kev be dead? We just spoke the other day.

Kev can't be dead. That's my boy since fifth grade.

I interrupted Dad. "Kevin? Kev? As in *Kevin Nicholas?*"

"Yes."

I mopped my face with my hand, slumped backward into my chair, stared at the floor, and blocked my old man out again.

Kev was only nineteen. Who dies at nineteen? Poor kids in the hood who get merked in drive-bys or young people with medical conditions. Kev didn't belong in either group.

His family wasn't balling out *MTV Cribs* rich, but they had loot. Kev was captain of our high-school cross-country team with diesel Spider-Man arms, abs, and crazy-dumb strength and speed. I still remember the time in our school parking lot when he sprinted, dove in the air, and front-flipped over the hood of Mick's car.

Dad's face turned sadder as he reached for me.

My body moved on auto, snatching my hand away from his, flicking my earbud out, standing, and leaving him behind as he shouted, "Will, if you need to talk, I'm here!"

I headed upstairs and punched my bedroom door

open. I suddenly felt I needed to see some of the SC with this news about Kev. I wondered if they knew about him already. If yeah, I bet they needed to see me, too.

I walked to my bookshelf and slid Kev's senior yearbook off and opened to page 23 to us and five other members of the SC in our team photo. We were bodybuilder posing and flexing in our tank tops and shorts after a race we'd won. We were smirking, nodding, and winking—all cocky—as if we were in that LMFAO video going, "Wiggle, wiggle, wiggle, wiggle." We all wore workout wristbands with our school's name over the middle of our left forearms. People always asked why we wore them whenever we had on T-shirts. We never answered, and they figured it was some weird schoolpride style of ours.

We thought nothing could hurt us. I huffed and stared at him. *What happened, Kev? You should've been the last of us to die, not the first.*

Back in the day, I used to feel everyone in the SC was the same: mostly white, some mixed (like me, Mick, Kev, and Vince), pissed with good reasons, jocks, and dumb enough to risk everything, sometimes our lives, doing dangerous stuff. I never told anyone, but I knew Kev wasn't like me or any of us.

He was . . . better—even though he was straight evil at times.

He had something we didn't: cult-leader charisma.

Dude was half magnet, half sponge. Me, Candy, Mick, and a lot of kids couldn't help but be drawn to Kev, and once we did we got sponged up.

I flicked the yearbook to page 57 and saw me, Kev, and most of the SC in a photo where the school crammed us into the gym for a big, all-school shot. We all surrounded Kev, and almost none of our separate personalities were in this picture because we wore our hair, shirts, and jeans like each other—like Kev.

I shut the yearbook and in the blink of an eye I flashed back to the night of that photo and our first blood initiation.

"I'm out," Mick said. "You doing this, Will?"

I nodded.

"You guys *officially* are clowns." Mick stormed into the night.

Jake nervously bit his fingernails. "I'm throwing Mick a beat-down if he tells anyone."

"Easy, J," Kev told Jake. "Everyone here knows Mick'll lay you out if you step to him. Mick's a mutt, not a butt."

It bugged me a little when Kev called Mick and mixed people mutts, because I'm mixed. Besides, Kev's mixed, too. But he didn't say it a lot and I didn't get bent out of shape about racist remarks the way Mick did. Maybe because I could pass for white; Mick obviously had an A-Rod look going on.

As for Jake, he didn't like hearing Kev say Mick would crush him in a fight (even though we all knew it was true), so he started posturing the way cops and cowboys do. He grabbed and jostled his belt buckle, shifting his eyes from left to right while thinking of a comeback. Kev took the hot air out of Jake's balloon before he puffed up too much by saying, "J, chill." He stared at me. "Mick's no snitch. Right, Will?"

I thought back to the summer in grade school when me, Mick, and Kev first met. "William Benedict. Michael Galindo. Candace Lomack. Kevin Nicholas." Father H read our names off his clipboard. "Take a few seconds to introduce yourselves. You're doing altar attendant training together." From that minute to now, Kev and Mick had had a roller-coaster friendship, and Kev did a lot to turn Mick into a ticking time-bomb. Like my freshman year, when Kev rode Mick for being nice to his Latina house cleaner. "When your old man split for Jersey, you should've sent your Hispanic side with him. Stop relating to immigrants, *comprende?*" That and other moments should've made Mick explode, leak stuff, and crap all over Kev's squeaky-clean reputation, but Mick never did. Maybe because he knew Kev had dirt on him, too. Maybe because Mick knew that airing Kev's dirty laundry would mean hanging me and all the whole SC out for the police to scoop us up. I didn't know his reasons, but Mick kept our secrets.

I reassured Jake and the rest of the SC. "Mick's good. He won't say anything."

Kev flashed Jake his electric smile, which could light up all those buildings in those Manhattan skyline pictures. You could see Jake's tension begin to melt off him as his jerky right shoulder stopped moving and he winked at Kev. Kev had this way of making people feel ant-small, like right now with J. Then he'd turn on his charm and people forgot their beefs with him.

Kev turned back to the fireplace and, with both hands in grill gloves, pulled out two branding irons and stared at their red-hot tips as he twisted them super slow and smiled at the half-inch-square glowing initials on each end: *SC.* His dark basement, with window shades down and halogen lamps on low, made Kev's intense eyes and smile seem wicked and made the sizzling *S* and *C* brands glow neon-bright. His basement had a bunch of branding irons, from *A* to *Z* in all sizes, from when his grandfather, Poppy Nicholas, branded horses in his stable. While eyeing the branding irons, Kev started talking loud enough for the whole SC to hear. He said everyone in our group had a broken family story that made us pieces of a puzzle that fit together. Kev's dad had committed suicide. My mom had cracked up and spent the rest of her life in a mental hospital. All of us had demons, Kev said, and our crew was our haven, but as tight as we sometimes were, we still were only puzzle pieces that came together once in a while.

"We need something that bonds us forever." Kev stepped into the center of the room with the brands, and we formed a circle around him. I couldn't take my eyes off the neon *S* and *C,* the way I was both attracted to and scared of the lava of that Hawaii volcano that my dad and I visited during our Big Island vacation.

At the start of his senior year, when Kev told me his idea about branding ourselves with *S*s and *C*s, I thought he was kidding. Four or five months ago when he showed me the hot-iron brands, I still didn't believe him. But now I knew he'd meant every word of it.

As crazy as brands sounded, everyone in our crew wanted their brand more than they didn't for a few reasons. First, proving we weren't punks was always on our minds. The SC had enough street connects to know who did illegal tattoos. We could've plopped the cash down and gotten tatted up, but tats were soft compared to manning up and letting hot iron press into your flesh without squealing like a baby. Second, every Joe, Bob, and guy in between on the planet, from mechanics to drug dealers to athletes to entertainers to presidents of countries, had tattoos. Tats were supposed to be gangster, but they were becoming boardroom: neat, pretty, and elite. Not brands. You knew in a room of thirty tattoo-wearing dudes that probably none of them had nutted up and gotten a brand. Plus, to get a brand, you couldn't walk into a shop and buy one like a computer app or a pair of sneakers. The branding had to happen underground, and brands had underground swag. It was an initiation. We also agreed we needed to put the brand somewhere on our bodies that showed we lived up to the rep of our crew's name.

When we were younger, me and Kev had talked after his father blew his brains out, around the same time my mom had the nervous breakdown that broke my family apart.

Me and Kev agreed, back then, that his father and my mother had tried pleasing people too much and that had led them over the edge. Right there, me and Kev made a promise not to play the people-pleasing game and live life in fear. We agreed to kill the part of ourselves that was weak, that played it safe and cared about people's reactions. "We should make our little crew official," Kev smiled his megawatt smile that made me feel good, "and give ourselves a name. How about the Suicide Crew?" I grinned back.

Since that day, Kev and I had carefully invited kids into the SC who wanted to bury the worst parts of their families and themselves. Kids who could keep secrets, had big fight in them, and wanted to chump death and people who we felt were dying before they died. Every year we added a new guy who wasn't a punk-ass to the

SC. They proved themselves through two sets of initiations: death-defying dares and assaults on well-to-do jerks. Drinking parties with proof-through-the-roof bottles of alcohol plus break-ins to steal prized trophies of gopher-adults we hated were the softer felonies on our growing list of crimes. Every new badass in our group just made our crew even more hungry to do the next-level thing for us to get stamped 100 Percent Grade A SC-Approved Fearless.

Now here Kev was shifting our gears to the next NEXT level with the SC brand. We, including Matthew, Vick, Vince, Jason, Trevor, Scott, and Jake, agreed that the SC brand had to be burned on the inside of our left forearms and anyone who screamed like a toddler during his brand was getting his face smeared with the dog crap Vince had brown-bagged from his German shepherd. Plus, Mr. Crybaby would have to drink two ounces of piss from a random group member.

"Do me." Kev stared straight into my eyes. "Then I do you. After, everyone chooses who brands them."

"Me?" I asked. "You want me to brand you?"

"Man up, Will. You and me started the SC. It has to be you." Kev turned away from me, went to the fireplace, and set the irons in the flames, then pulled his grill gloves and shirt off. "Take them pokers out in a minute. I'll be at the bar, and I don't want a blindfold. I want to see and feel it burn."

All you could hear in the room was the sound of fire crackling.

I had to admit it to myself: I had thought Kev was playing about the brands, even up to now.

Then this thought hit me: Was this my initiation? Was Kev testing me to see if I had the balls to go through with this?

He went straight to the bar, poured his mom's Jack into a coffee cup until it was half full, gurgled it down, and winced while giving me a thumbs-up. It always bugged me out how his mom left her alcohol accessible when she left for her exotic weekend getaways with her housewife friends.

The thought came to me again: *Kev won't let you brand him. He's punking you. The whole SC is quizzing you.*

I slowly walked up to the fireplace and stared into the flames; the unbearable heat that made me squint. I could also feel everyone's stares drilling holes through the back of my skull. All eyes were on me because the guy branding had to man up as much as the guy getting the brand.

What if he's serious and wants me to burn him? The one time I put something hot on someone's skin was when I accidentally swiped my index finger when I ironed my clothes in middle school. And the pain! That was intense. I wondered how a hot iron, straight on skin on purpose for a few seconds, would feel. The idea made my stomach turn into a desktop wave machine, but I fought to hide my queasiness.

What if Kev was trying to herb me? The idea of me being seen as a chump by the SC made me angry. These dudes looked to me for leadership; I wasn't about to fall off and down the ladder and become the butt of their jokes. "Soft." "Punk." I imagined them hissing those names at me, and it got me mad. I took that anger and violently grabbed and slid on the grill gloves, snatched the brand irons out of the flames, and headed over to Kev fast to show I had elephant-size cojones. *Everybody wants to play me? They should play lotto.*

I stomped toward Kev, and everyone rode my ass right to him, thirsty to see.

As I got to Kev, Scott bumped into Vick, who then bumped into me and the fiery brand tips almost stabbed into Kev's mom's Venetian rug. I swung around. "Back up. Y'all stupid? You gonna burn Kev's house down!"

Kev snapped at me. "Will, keep focused. Do this already!" He crazy-cult-leader-eyed me, and I knew this wasn't a test to see if I'd punk out. Kev was dead serious. This was our next initiation.

My stomach did a desktop-wave-machine flip again. I wasn't sure how to handle a hot-iron brand.

Kev probably read my indecision and confusion from my tense expression. "Just lay the *S* down as even as you can, Will," he said in his most soothing voice. "The *C* after will be easier. You'll see. Right now, just go in gentle and even. You not careful and stamp down too hard and that iron'll melt through my skin into my muscle."

I laid the *C* brand on Kev's mom's marble bar counter and licked a trail of salty sweat that trickled onto my lips. I was sweating bullets, and you'd think it was from the heat of the fireplace or the red-hot brands in my hands, but nope, the sweat was from fear. I looked at Kev, and his eyes were locked on his forearm as if he could already see his *S* and *C* there. I also tried picturing seeing the initials on his forearm to help me not mess up. Man, you could hear every guy breathing in the room. The scene was filled with so much silence and tension that if I turned around and yelled "BOO!" at that exact moment, every SC member would have had a fatal heart attack.

I raised the hot-iron *S* a foot away from Kev's arm to see if he'd pull away, but he didn't flinch. I moved the neon-hot tip closer and closer to his skin. In my heart, I wished someone would interrupt and stop this craziness, but I wasn't going to be the one doing the stopping. There is an ancient Chinese proverb: "The nail that sticks out gets hammered." I had the hot-iron *S* three inches away from Kev's soft inner forearm flesh, which seemed as pure as a newborn's tummy. Then Kev spoke.

"Remember when we named ourselves the SC, Will?"

"Yeah." I paused and smiled and wished we could zip

back there to when we were slightly innocent kids and before we did sick junk like this.

"Kill that weak part of you," Kev said. "Brand me."

"Yeah," I gulped. "On three."

"Bet."

Me and Kev said in beat, "One, two . . . THREE!"

I leaned the hot-iron brand in fast but not too hard, and it took every cell in my body not to close my eyes as I heard and saw the crackle and hiss of Kev's skin as the flesh around the curves of the S darkened and bubbled up. Pus. Blood. Some clear liquid ran down his arm.

"HOLY . . . !" Kev shouted, then held back saying anything else as he bit his lip and stared at the ceiling. He fought to stay as still as possible so he didn't mess up his brand. His blue eyes glowed bluer, hot, as if the flames from the fireplace were flowing through the brand and into him and light-bulb lighting up his insides. I didn't know why I knew, but I knew I had to take the brand off immediately so I did. As much as I wanted to puke at the sight of the S that disfigured Kev's forearm, I simultaneously felt good at seeing it and how cool it looked and knowing that the first and hardest part of me branding Kev was behind me.

Kev pushed me aside, raced to the sink, turned the faucet on, and shoved his arm under the streaming water. He stomped one foot and cursed worse than I ever heard. But never once did he cry. Me, Jason, and

Trevor rushed to comfort him, but Kev held his hand up and waved us off.

"Chill," he exhaled. "I'm . . . good. I'm good."

Slowly, he brought his arm out from under the water. First he admired the handiwork, then he raised his arm for us all to see. We might as well have been in that movie *300,* because everyone but me spotted his *S* and raised their fists and shouted, "YEAAAAHHHHH!" Me and Kev locked eyes, and I felt this incredible energy flowing between us. It was a closeness to him I had never had before. Of all the guys, he trusted me to brand him. Anytime he saw his brand, he would have to think of me. Whenever I saw his brand, I'd have the secret knowing, "I did that." The other SC members were saying stuff like, "Kev's badass," "Kev took that straight up," "Kev's the man," and "SC forever." It was demented, but Kev had been right before when he'd said we all were just puzzle pieces and a brand would bond our crew for life.

"You need to reheat that." Kev pointed to the brand with the *C*. "Can't have an *S* without a *C,* right?"

I looked over and saw that it was dimming. It could burn skin, but it wouldn't appear as nice as the *S*.

I grabbed the *C* brand and turned toward the fireplace, and all the guys in the SC parted and cleared a path for me to fire it up.

As I stepped toward the flames, I checked my G-Shock watch and made out the time: 11:42 p.m.

In less than ten minutes, it would be my turn to be burned.

In an hour, we'd all be drunk, admiring each other's SC brands, bragging, and planning the next NEXT **NEXT** level initiation.

A knock rocked my bedroom door at the same moment that my cell rang, and I was snapped out of my memory of our brandings. I was still holding the yearbook. I was still standing alone in my room in front of my shelf. Kev was still dead.

"Will?" my dad yelled from behind my shut door. "Will? Are you okay?"

I managed a "Yeah."

"I ordered in food," Dad said. "Come get some when you're ready."

"Sure thing."

He left, and I went and picked up my cell and checked to see whose name was on the screen. It was Josh, one of the guys from the SC. I hit IGNORE.

Suddenly, I remembered some of the next levels me and Kev had discussed that last night that we wanted the SC to go through together.

The phone rang again, and I spied the screen, thinking it was Josh again. It wasn't; it was Mick. Maybe Mick had been smart to get out of the SC on the night of our brands. I hit IGNORE on Mick, too.

I rolled up my fleece's left sleeve and stared at the *SC* burned into the soft flesh of my inside forearm.

Kev came up with the SC.

He created the staircase of our dumb-dare initiations, and with him gone, I knew the SC would be expecting our next steps from me. Right now, I couldn't even think about Kev being dead. Forget about thinking about next SC steps without him.

I ran my fingers over my *S* and *C. Man, what happened, Kev? You should've been the last of us to die, not the first.*

RUNNING MAN

CHARLES R. SMITH JR.

MARCO STOOD PANTING at his door as his key twisted the lock open. Before he could get to the ice-cold Gatorade that was his reward for a ten-mile run, his phone dinged. He ignored it and cracked the bottle open. One purple sip in, and the phone dinged again. And again. And again. And again.

"What the hell, man?" he snapped.

He rushed to the counter, looked at the phone, and saw sixteen texts waiting. "Somebody die or something?" He half laughed before scrolling through the messages. Most were from his old high-school cross-country teammates.

Sure ur out on run but hit me up when u get in. Big news.

Yo M, where u at?

Check ur vm running man

Left u a msg and e-mailed u too M. Where tf u at? Holla back

Marco WTF man get back to me

Yooooooooooooo u hear about Kev?

Marco scrolled through more, furious now. What about Kev?

The answer came in the next text from his buddy Will.

Funeral is this Friday let me know if u r coming.

Funeral? Marco went through each text, and a clear picture emerged. His old cross-country captain and running buddy, Kevin Nicholas, was dead. Suicide was the rumor. He gulped a purple swig and made his way into his room.

Marco plopped onto his bed and stared, open-mouthed, at a picture of him and Kevin in their team tank tops. They both thrust a number-one finger at the camera, Marco all smiles, hair tousled, sweat beaded on his forehead; Kevin stone-faced, no sweat, hair untouched as if he had gone for a walk in the park.

"Damn," Marco muttered to the boy in the photo, "what happened, Kev?"

He drained the bottle and hurled it at the pillow on his bed.

"Fuuuuuuuuuuuuuccccccccck!" he shouted. "I gotta get outta here."

And just like that, Marco was back on the pavement, retracing his and Kev's favorite running route. His usual quick, steady gait—the one that had earned him a state title and a full ride to St. John's—was gone, replaced by herky-jerky stutter steps. The rhythmic breathing pattern that Kev used to tease him about—"Yo, you sound like a girl getting pounded"—was gone, replaced by staccato exhales.

Marco herky-jerked himself to the outskirts of the park, and just as he was ready to collapse on the nearest bench, Kevin's voice rang in his ear: "Stop being a bitch and just keep running."

Just keep running, Marco.

Past the church. Past Candy's house. Past the Chinese food spot. Past the pizza spot. Past the pawnshop. Past the check-cashing spot.

"Hold up," Kevin said one particular early-Monday-morning run.

He motioned Marco to an alley behind the pizza spot. "Follow me."

Kevin led the way down the alley, past the pizza spot, and behind the pawnshop. Marco followed in his footsteps. Kevin's slow walk sped up to a light jog as he called out to Marco.

"You think you can outrun a bullet?"

"What?" Marco said.

"I said," Kevin hissed, "you think you can outrun a bullet?"

As Kevin picked up his jog, Marco noticed someone approach the back entrance of the pawnshop. A guard with a black satchel in his hand and a gun on his hip banged on the metal door.

"Come on," Kevin called.

He burst into a sprint, usually reserved for the final kick of a cross-country race. But this was different. Kevin's sprint had purpose. He bolted toward the guard and smothered him as he reached for his holster. A knee to the groin dropped the stocky guard, and a left upper-cut to the chin laid him on his back.

Kevin snatched the satchel and took off down the alley. Marco bolted after him. The squawk of a radio broke through the squish of their sneakers on the pavement. The boys left the pizza spot in the rearview and raced past the Chinese food spot next door.

KA-RACK! A bullet pinged off a Dumpster behind them.

Kevin darted left. Marco darted right. Another bullet whizzed behind them. Kevin clutched the satchel to his chest and kicked into second gear. Marco swiveled his head back at the guard, then did the same.

"What's in the bag, Kev?"

"Just keep running!"

And they did. Past the shoe store. Past the Jamaican beef patty spot. Past the library. Past the market. Past

Will's house. Into the park. Up Slog Hill. So named because you had to slog through a path of waist-high weeds and crushed beer cans to sit on top of the rock overlooking the cemetery and the city in the distance.

The satchel dropped from Kev's shoulder with a soft clang. The two hovered over the bag, panting quickly. Every few breaths, their breathing slowed until they were both silent.

"You almost got us killed back there!" Marco said.

"But I didn't."

Kevin stared at Marco, then dropped his eyes to the satchel. He ripped the zipper open and jammed his right hand inside. His eyes drifted up as if he were reaching into a grab bag. He pulled out an oily gray cloth, wrapped around something like a small gift. Then he peeled back the gray petals of the cloth, and a shimmer of silver peeked out. Like a child, Kevin snatched the cloth away and revealed a sleek, palm-sized, silver pistol. He palmed it and turned it over in his hands, inspecting it.

"Damn," Kevin said. "I already got one of these in black. I was hoping for some *Dirty Harry*–type shit."

"Wait, you already have a gun?"

"Actually, two," Kevin said. He flipped open the chamber, gave it a spin, then flipped it shut. "The black one and a broke nine-millie."

"So what do you need another one for?" Marco asked. "Especially a hot one."

"What do you care?" Kevin said.

"Seeing as how I got shot at after you bum-rushed that guard, I very much care," Marco said. "What do you need three guns for?"

"Two guns," Kevin corrected him. "One's broken."

"What the hell you even need ONE gun for?"

"Protection."

"Protection? This ain't the Bronx. What you need protection from?"

Kevin looked through Marco.

"Myself."

A grin crept across Kevin's mouth, and he laughed it off.

"But seriously," Kevin started, "the fifteenth is coming up, which means the check-cashing place will be hopping. So I was thinking . . ."

"You was thinking nothing," Marco said. "I ain't robbing nobody. Especially with a hot gun." He hopped off the rock. "Man, how you sound?"

Kevin stared off into the distance at the cemetery. His eyes wandered southeast, where no headstones or crosses lay. But his father did.

"We gotta take this thing back," Marco said. "Knock on the door and take off or something."

"Naw, Running Man," Kevin said, very cool. "That's not how this is going down." He hopped off the rock and thrust the gun at Marco's eyes.

"Get that outta my face," Marco said.

"Why?" Kevin inched in. "You scared?"

Marco turned his head left to ignore Kevin. And the gun.

"Come on, M," Kev said, the grin reemerging, "I ain't gonna shoot it. Trust me."

Marco glanced back at him.

"You do trust me, don't you?" Kev said.

Marco stared off to his right.

"Relax, Running Man." Kev lowered the gun. "I haven't done shit yet."

"Yet?"

"You know what I mean. I got a plan."

Marco listened to Kevin break down how he planned to take all three guns, walk into a police precinct, and turn them in for cash.

"Three guns'll get you three-hunny. No questions," Kevin said with a grin.

"And then what?"

Kev lifted the gun again and stepped toward Marco.

"You ask a lot of questions, Running Man."

Marco's hands flew into the air like he was about to get mugged. Kevin could make you feel that way.

"You really need to chill, M." Kevin let out a sinister laugh. "I told you it ain't loaded."

Loaded or not, Marco hated the cold steel staring him down.

Kevin lowered the gun and leaned against the rock. "With three bills, I can get me a clean piece," he said. "A four-five. One of them sleek silver-and-black joints."

His eyes lit up like a kid detailing what he wanted most for Christmas.

Marco shook his head. "You still gonna hit the check-cashing spot?"

"You don't even worry about that, Running Man," Kevin said. He pushed off the rock and slung his arm, with the gun dangling, around Marco's neck and pulled his ear close. "You just worry about keeping your mouth shut about all of this."

The words echoed in Marco's head as he picked up his pace in the park. The scent of stale beer assaulted his nose. Slog Hill was just around the curve. Cans crunched and crinkled as he panted his way through the tall weeds. He climbed onto the rocks, lay spread-eagled on his back, and stared at the summer clouds.

Marco hadn't been on Slog Hill or this rock since he'd sat right there with Kevin, trying to talk him out of a robbery that was probably never gonna happen. Kevin, pulling one last bait and switch.

A slow exhale escaped Marco's mouth. A deep breath filled his lungs and lifted his chest.

"Keep running, Kev."

MAKING UP THE DEAD

NORA RALEIGH BASKIN

OF COURSE, it isn't his age that makes me think of Barry. This body is young. Nineteen, the card reads. Kevin Nicholas.

Suicide, Nadira, Sampson told me. *So make him look as good as you can.*

Maybe it's the color of this body's hair, the distinct cocoa of his skin. And maybe it's something more than that. I like to think that when a body is dead it can't lie anymore and all that is left is the truth. So I make up stories as I am filing the nails of stiff-fingered dead people, putting on foundation or lipstick, or combing their hair. I try to imagine who they were and if they can (or should) be forgiven for what they did in their lives. I want to believe there are good people and bad people and that in the end we all get what we deserve, but the dead always remind us that is not true.

Sampson wants me to make this body tell a lie. He wants me to make this body, this boy, look the best I can, so that no one will be reminded that he took his own life. What was it, Kevin, that was so terrible you couldn't go on? Do you wish now you had another chance?

People don't realize how much work goes into my job. I am like a plastic surgeon for the dead. I can plump up your lips and smooth out your wrinkles. I just need to get in there before the embalming fluid starts to harden.

Are you sorry you succeeded?

Was your pain greater than all others?

I mean, we all feel pain, don't we? Well, maybe not all of us.

Mom?

Everything I did, I did for you.

I smoked weed for the first time. I shaved my legs. I shoplifted at a local grocery store when our camp took a field trip into town. I kissed a boy and I let him feel me up. I wanted you to love me, Mom, and if that meant I had to get Barry to want me, well, then, I could do that, too.

And so with everything I did for the first time, I dreamed about how I would tell you and I dreamed about how proud you would be of me. I was practically glowing with the anticipation of being the daughter you really wanted. Instead of who I was.

The daughter you didn't want.

How funny, I would have told you when you came at the end of that summer to pick me up—that's nearly ten years ago—*how funny that I didn't want to come here at all.* How I resisted and begged you to let me stay home. I was so afraid of losing you. I was so afraid that if I went away for a month, you'd finally decide you didn't want me anymore and I wouldn't be there to talk you out of it.

I am too much trouble, too difficult, a handful. Isn't that what Barry said about me? A handful? A pill? A pain in the ass? Isn't that why he hits me, because I am asking for it? "You bet you'll never do that again"—as he drags me by the hair up the stairs.

But now look at me, I thought at summer camp a month later. *I am one of you. I am nearly twelve years old. It's not too late. Things can only get better from here on. I can't wait to tell you about my summer.*

First, I will tell you about Danny, the boy who slipped his hand under my T-shirt as we lay in the grass under the shooting stars. There was nothing there, nothing but small fleshy bumps, less than Caroline Behar had in third grade because she was fat. The other kids would make fun of her behind her back, and to her face, saying she had boobs. When Danny's fingers were on my belly, it took everything I had not to laugh out loud.

It tickled. My whole body was rising and tightening with goose pimples. I could feel his skin on my skin, under my shirt, over my chest, touching my nipples and making me want to die laughing.

But I didn't. I didn't because I knew this was what grown-ups did. It was what you and Barry did, and somehow I knew that if I did it, too, you would like me more. Barry would like me more. And you would let me stay with you.

Barry is dark, but it's not his skin that's dark—although he is honey colored, chestnut, cappuccino, mocha tan. It is his face that is dark. His eyes. It is the inside of his eyes. It is the air that moves around him, moves with him. It is the dark that I become when I am near him.

Stephen likes him. As soon as they met, they were fast friends.

"Why do I have to go to camp and Stephen doesn't?" I asked you even though I already knew the answer. You were doing the dishes when you dropped the bomb. You told me you had already talked to Dad and he had agreed to pay for it. Why would you ask Dad for anything? You always talk about horrible he was, how he treated you, how selfish and thoughtless he was. When you got divorced and he moved back to Queens Village to live with his parents, with Gigi and Pops, you made fun of him. You said he'd never get past his past, but when he can pay to send me away for the summer, you call him right up.

"Maybe if you spent more time worrying about your-self and not your brother, you'd be better off," you told me. You turned off the hot water and dried your hands on a dish towel.

"I don't want to go, Mom. Please, don't make me."

Out of sight, out of mind. They would forget about me if I went away. They would see they didn't need me, didn't want me.

Then, in a softer moment, you went on: "Besides, you might like it there. You'll make friends. Some people make lifelong friends at sleepaway camp. Then they grow up and say it was the best part of their childhood. I want you to have something I never could."

"Please, Mommy. Please." She didn't hear me.

"Besides, all Jewish kids go to summer camp," she said.

"You didn't." She didn't answer me.

But I am not Jewish. I am not black. I am something in between, something that doesn't belong anywhere.

I don't want anything you didn't have, I want to cry. *Just leave him, Mom. Just leave Barry, and it will be the three of us again. You, and me, and Stephen, and maybe Daddy will take us back.*

Danny was younger than me by two months. He had just turned eleven in July and he was smaller than me, but unlike me, he had blond hair and blond-person skin. Danny was young and light, and I don't know why, but he was kind to me. We sat in the very last row in the bus, close together, talking, while the other campers dove into their temporarily returned smartphones with maniacal focus. Most of the other kids were going to go to the movies or the mall. There was a counselor to accompany each group. For every twelve kids, there was one counselor. Danny and I planned on sneaking away by telling the mall counselor, Amy, that we were going to the movies and telling the movie counselor, Mark, that we wanted to shop at the mall.

"Fine, Nadira," Amy said. "Just make sure you let Mark know you are in his group. And while you're at it, remind him we all need to be back at the bus by nine thirty." It was that easy.

"What do you want to do?" I asked Danny. We were free. I was free. I was far away from Barry, from my brother, from my dad, even from you in that moment, but I was all right. The summer night was magic. The sun was already slipping away from the sky, turning the world a yellowish red. The moon was rising like a wondrous gift for all to see but no one to touch and no one to ruin. The sticky August warmth stayed in the air even as shadows overtook the light, and Danny took my hand.

"Let's go to the store and get candy," he said.

"I don't have money. Do you?"

"No," Danny admitted.

Neither one of us had the unlimited canteen access that some of the other campers had, to buy envelopes and paper and stamps, candy and drinks, to take out cash for shopping in town. Cell phones had been returned, but for this field trip only. Danny and I were the only two campers who didn't have one to begin with.

Neither Danny nor I had any money. We had each other.

"I know a way," Danny told me.

And Danny explained it to me. He told me how to walk the aisles, how to look and how to sound, how we could work together, one of us talking to the cashier while the other would drop packages of candy into our pockets. It was wrong, and it was scary, and when I had done it, when Danny and I were running down the street as fast as we could, our pockets stuffed with Kit Kats and Sour Patch Kids, I knew I would tell you all about Danny. Maybe not about the stealing, because you wouldn't like that. And Daddy *really* wouldn't like that. A black kid has to be better than everyone else. He can't even walk out of a deli without his soda in a bag and a receipt in his hand.

But I did it for you, Mom.

Danny didn't know anything about Barry, of course. At camp, we could be anything we wanted, and given enough time—like a whole month—it became true. Barry's darkness had turned into a dream that I couldn't remember having. Did he punch me in the stomach when I left my crayons on the floor and Stephen and his friends stepped on them, grinding them into the wood? Or when I left the dog food uncovered in the refrigerator? I couldn't remember if you had been there watching when I doubled over in pain. I had only the vaguest memory of sitting on the toilet seat, looking up at the unfinished ceiling, the wires, blue and red and yellow, leading off in all sorts of places. Pipes and exposed wood and pink insulation. I couldn't breathe. No air could get into my lungs. It was only a matter of time before I would die. I looked up into the ceiling that was supposed to be there but wasn't, and I knew, yes, I was going to die. I was going to die, and if I could have breathed, I would have laughed. I would have laughed because there was nothing left to do.

But slowly the air came back in, my heart slowed down, and I didn't die after all, and nothing was very funny, just another part of a confusing dream.

Danny and I were sweating, panting hard. We rested our hands on our knees and tried to catch our breath. We were far enough away from the grocery store, clutching our bounty. We were safe.

"What time is it?" I asked.

"I don't know," Danny answered. We sat down on the curb to inspect our contraband and then eat it.

"Well, as long as we are back at the bus by nine thirty."

With our bellies full and our teeth stinging from sugar, we lay back down on the grass beside the street and waited for the night to darken and the shooting stars to come out. Where were we? Vermont? Maine? Upstate New York? I don't remember where the camp was, and I probably didn't know in the first place. I knew it took hours to get there. Dad drove me up, but we didn't talk much.

What would I tell him anyway?

Dad, I don't like Mom's boyfriend. He is dark and bearded. He doesn't shower, and he smells bad. He smells dark. He smokes a lot of weed, like all the time, like first thing in the morning and last thing at night. Something is wrong. Something is wrong with me, so he hits me and he scares me. But maybe that's why you left, Dad, without saying anything. So if I tell you and you don't do anything, that would be worse. If I tell you and you don't believe me, I could lose you both.

Don't bite the hand that feeds you.

Don't bite the hand.

Don't bite.

So why am I always biting everyone?

■ ■ ■

But now it's all different. Now I've shaved my legs and smoked weed with Morgan in Omega Cabin instead of going to arts and crafts. I stole candy from the grocery store and I am in love with Danny, just like you are in love with Barry.

"Really, the best time to see shooting stars is just before dawn," Danny told me.

"Really?"

"Yeah, my dad told me that when we went camping one summer."

I was quiet. The grass was wet and cold, but I didn't move. I think I knew if I stayed quiet, Danny would kiss me.

"Yeah, it has something to do with our orbital motion through space and being on the tail end of the meteors. That's what they are, you know? Shooting stars. They're meteors that are moving faster than we are." Danny lifted himself onto his elbows.

"Oh."

And Danny leaned over and kissed me.

We didn't open our mouths or anything like that, but we kissed. I know it. He rested his body on top of mine, sort of to the side so he wouldn't hurt me, but so that I would feel his warmth and smell the clean scent of his clothing and the boyish scent of his skin. I let him touch me because it felt good and safe, and because it made me want to laugh.

"I love you, Nadira," he told me.

"I love you, too."

"We should probably get going."

"We should. Want my last bag of Skittles?"

"Sure," Danny said. "We can share."

"You're going to be a woman soon, Nadira," she told me just before I left for camp. I hadn't gotten my period yet, and I wouldn't for another year and a half, but somehow I knew that wasn't what she was talking about.

"You're going to be a very lovely young woman." She was working on my hair, which wasn't quite like hers but took a lot of work. I held back my tears as she pulled and twisted. "Barry's going to notice it, too. I'm going to have to watch out for you, aren't I?"

"I don't want to go. Please, Mom," I said.

She kissed the top of my head. It was the last time.

What did I know? I really have to ask myself. Did I somehow know when I left for camp that I would never see you again? That just before the last day, the director would find me.

"Is this Nadira Washington?" he would ask Amy or Amber or Austin, or whatever my counselor's name was.

"Yeah, this is Nadira."

And then the director would turn to me. "Your father called. He says there's been some problem with your mother driving up here and he wants you to catch a ride back to New York with another family. Do you know Debra Klein?"

I didn't, but it would be Debra's mother and father who would squeeze me and all my stuff—except my pillow—into their SUV and drive us all the way back to New York City. We met my dad, and not you, at the rest stop just off the thruway. He thanked the Kleins and tried to offer them money for their trouble, but I don't remember if they took it or not, and when we got into his car, my dad told me that I would be living with him now. So he didn't exactly take us back, but he got stuck with me again.

You were gone. You took Stephen, because he is not a pill, but not me.

Now I have this thought and it is so funny, it is so hysterically funny I have to laugh out loud. I know I'm not supposed to really laugh when I am down here. This isn't exactly the kind of work environment where there is a lot of laughing going on. You never know when clients could be around.

Not that Sampson would ever fire me. He's got the hots for me. It's so obvious, it's pathetic. But still, it's disrespectful to be joyful when people are in mourning.

But imagine, Mom, can you just imagine if this *was* Barry lying here, naked and dead, and helpless and powerless? I can see the anger coming from his skin and floating harmlessly away into the air. I can see the darkness of his eyes, though they are glued shut and two eye caps are fitted carefully underneath. I look at his hands, and I can envision them balled into fists. But they can't hurt me now.

And neither can you.

I saw you one more time, at the women's clinic in Queens County. You were there with a friend and didn't seem to recognize me. But why would you? Five years had passed and you didn't look much different, but I was sixteen, not eleven. *I am a woman now, Mom, a pregnant one, with five hundred dollars in my pocket to pay for my troubles.*

Your friend was shaking and crying, and you seemed pretty occupied with calming her down. You didn't even notice me, sitting across from you in the waiting room. I knew a little bit about you, from Stephen when he would come to visit, which wasn't often. You and Barry split up, and you were with someone else now. A cross-country truck driver, I think I heard. Or a florist, or maybe it was a florist first and then the truck driver, I'm not sure.

The seats were cozy. There were happy pictures up in the waiting room, but your friend couldn't stop sobbing. I guessed she was there for the same thing I was. Then, at one point while your friend continued to sob, you looked up and right at me.

You knew who I was — *you must have.* But you didn't say a thing. You turned your eyes away quickly and looked down. How lucky that the nurse came out and called your friend's name. I watched you hurry away, through the door, into the doctor's office, without saying a thing.

So I will say it for you: *Nadira, I am so sorry. I was so wrong for letting you go. For leaving you. Please forgive me. It was not your fault. You were never too difficult. Please forgive me for hurting you. You never deserved that. It's all going to be all right now.*

Now this body is ready to be dressed in the clothes given to us by his family and his wounds will be hidden forever. I have to let the laughter out. I've glued his eyes shut, brushed his brows, tweezed any stray hair.

The last thing I do is slip the dental cups inside Kevin's cheeks because as his skin shrinks and dehydrates, his mouth can open, and his teeth can show. Never let the teeth show, they taught us in mortuary school. A little superglue is all it takes and his lips are sealed forever.

Are you sorry you succeeded?

Was your pain greater than all others?

I can laugh out loud. I can cry and I can laugh. I can feel pain and I can feel joy. Kevin is lying here dead, and somewhere in the world, you are still walking around, Barry is still walking around and I don't care anymore.

Because I walked out of the clinic that day and I stopped wanting you. I stopped waiting for you. I stopped missing you. Forever. I never went through with it. I walked out of that clinic, and I have never looked back.

Because you, because my own mother, left me, but I'm still here.

I am alive.

TWO-A-DAYS

CHRIS BARTON

JACKSON WASN'T SURE what to expect as he pulled open the field house's bright-blue metal door, but he figured he was in for something. Ribbing, razzing, mild hazing, whatever the usual treatment is when a new guy—especially one known mainly for getting all As—joins the football team. What he got, though, as he scanned for his locker and finally found the one with DEETS on a strip of masking tape, was a whole lot of nothing much. Plenty of no-eye-contacts. A few nods. A smattering of mumbles.

The only piece of gear in his locker was a bright-yellow helmet. No shoulder pads? Jackson looked around. Nobody else had pads, either—just the gray shorts and T-shirts they'd shown up in. He set his backpack on a bench, took his rubber mouth guard out of a pocket, and attached its strap to the face mask as the other guys were doing. He put his backpack into the locker, closed the door, opened the door, took the backpack back out, fished around for his combination lock, put the back-pack back in, closed the door again, and locked it up.

"Damn, man—you got *big*."

Jackson didn't recognize the voice, but he knew an acknowledgment of his spring and summer growth spurt when he heard one. He spun around, a grin beginning to take over his face. It stopped, though, as soon as he real-ized that the words hadn't been spoken to him—and, in fact, had been spoken to someone whose flexed bicep, to say nothing of the rest of him, wasn't especially big.

"Huh," Jackson grunted softly. He'd been planning to scowl a lot this morning anyway—now he had a good reason. He turned to follow other players as they carried their helmets from the gale-force AC contained by the blue door out into the 86 degrees and thousand percent humidity of the Central Texas morning.

Jackson had never so much as watched a football practice, let alone participated in two of them in a single day. For months, his transformation from pudgy to strapping had promised a chance to stand out at Agarita High the same way his dad had thirty years earlier. He knew there was more to it than size, though. Now that he was here—one of dozens of boys in helmets milling about on the practice field—Jackson hoped he was tough enough, or at least looked it. He scowled again.

The problem was, he'd pictured himself swaggering around in pads that enhanced his new frame while his helmetless head left his face easily recognizable. Being outfitted in just the opposite way was not creating the Jackson 2.0 impression that he had hoped for. Those helmets made all the guys look pretty much the same, so anyone who hadn't already recognized Jackson wasn't likely to now.

The helmets did something else, too. The contrast between the players' large, helmeted heads and relatively slim, padless bodies made Jackson think of the single most startling skeleton on display at the natural history museum. To a certain kind of kid, it was hilarious. Jackson couldn't help himself.

"We look . . ." Jackson began whispering to the rangy boy next to him as the coaches approached the field. There was no acknowledgment that Jackson was speaking, so he started over. *"Dude,"* he hissed, and the other guy turned to him. "We look like *toddler skeletons!* Don't these helmets make us look like giant *toddlers?"*

Jackson's observation was met with blankness. Rangy didn't answer him, and a sudden flush of unease, a sense that he'd said something *unfootball,* began to rise up within Jackson. Or maybe Rangy was about to respond—his lips and eyebrows had all started moving

93

toward the center of his freckled face, as if a reply were forming—but then the coaches all blew their whistles at once.

Practice pretty much consisted of running and sweating. Sprints. Laps. Agility drills with lots of starting and stopping and changing directions whenever a coach whistled, which was constantly. Jackson's helmet wasn't even used for anything, really, other than getting him used to viewing the world through a face mask. Oh, and holding the mouthpiece, which Jackson soon realized he had put in upside down. Until he had a chance to reinstall it between gulps of Gatorade during a break, the mouthpiece kept twisting out of his mouth every time he relaxed his jaw.

Nobody said much to him the whole time, with the exception of a coach letting him know he'd be practicing with the linemen that afternoon. It was already 93 degrees by the time practice ended at nine a.m., so Jackson could only imagine how brutal it would feel by five. But maybe none of the linemen had overheard his idiotic comment about skeletons, so at least there was that to look forward to.

When Jackson got home, he had the place to himself, and would for about the next six hours. He made a couple of sandwiches, turned on his laptop, and began scrolling through his feed to see what he'd missed. It looked like it would be the usual—nada—until he saw the comment his cousin Anna had made on someone else's status: *Oh god. I'm so sorry. R.I.P. Kevin — gone too soon. (I just...*

That was where Anna's comment cut off in his feed. She just what? Who was Kevin? And how soon was too soon?

Jackson clicked through. Someone named Kevin had died somehow, and that was out of the ordinary. Death wasn't a topic that typically came up among the people that Jackson was friends with. In fact, Jackson himself had never even been to a funeral, so an out-of-the-ordinary statement like *R.I.P. Kevin — gone too soon* made him curious. He wanted the context.

The context, at least at first, was something that Jackson had to piece together for himself. Anna lived in New York, so Kevin was nobody that Jackson knew. And Anna had been the only person in Jackson's feed who was saying anything about anybody named Kevin, so he wasn't — hadn't been — anybody famous.

The original post (*R.I.P. to my brother Kevin*) had been made a couple of weeks earlier by someone named Lydia, with a cross for a profile picture. It didn't give Jackson much to go on. But in the meantime, right on up through this morning, there had been 176 comments — 176! — and each of the profile pictures that had an actual human showed someone around Jackson's own age. This Kevin guy must have been *young,* Jackson thought. And popular.

He got up from the table to get a glass of water. As he moved around the kitchen, Jackson kept his eyes on the screen of his laptop. If anyone else followed Anna's comment with one of their own, Jackson would see it as it happened. But by the time Jackson sat back down, nobody had.

Many had offered up condolences (*Im so sorry...*), memories (*that time we got branded...*), or expressions of shock (*Kev is DEAD?*). Some of the comments, however, were more cryptic — they seemed to be exchanging certain information with certain people about what had happened. On the one hand, it seemed kind of rude — disrespectful — for them to be having this sort of private conversation on the public thread a teenage girl had started about her brother's untimely passing. On the other hand, if Jackson could crack the code, he could be one of those people in the know. He could slip into this tribe.

Jackson scanned through, looking for clues. Nobody mentioned cancer or any other kind of sickness. There were no references to car wrecks or accidents of any sort. A lot of unfamiliar and unexplained names got tossed around — several commenters were especially concerned about whether someone named Candy had heard about Kevin. Jackson felt entirely in the dark until he came to the comment, *Does any body know where he got tha gun from?*

Even as Jackson mentally rearranged the question (*from where he got tha gun?*), goose pimples rose on his thighs and forearms. From there on, the comments tended to be a lot less discreet. Long after the picture had become clear, Jackson continued to read on through to the end of the thread. When he got back to Anna's *R.I.P. Kevin—gone too soon,* it startled him, as if he'd forgotten what had started him reading in the first place.

Jackson pushed his chair back and stood up. Now what?

He walked down the hall toward his room, slowed down as he approached the pulled-shut door, and stopped entirely with his hand hovering just a couple of inches from its surface. His mom had made a list of things Jackson was expected to get done between practices. He had lightly argued that he shouldn't have to do anything during that time except recuperate, and he had breezed past the list on the kitchen counter earlier. But maybe he'd at least take a look now.

Why would somebody kill himself?

"Jeez, Jackson—let the guy rest in peace," Jackson told himself as he picked up the list.

Move laundry into dryer (and, yes, start it, Smart Mouth). Water plants on patio. Pick up your floor enough to run Roomba. Agreeing to do the things on the list each day was part of the deal that Jackson had reached with Mom. He could quit his job at H-E-B at the end of July so that it wouldn't interfere with football or school, but only on that one condition.

Had Kevin had a job? What would happen at H-E-B if one of the sackers or checkers committed suicide? Not in the store—nothing like that—but at home after a shift or on a day off?

The laundry was easy enough. He'd do that now. It was all his stuff, anyway. No way did he feel like doing anything outside, though, not even in the shade of the patio. And what was the point in having a robot vacuum cleaner if you had to pick stuff up out of its way? His room was a mess, sure, but it wasn't bothering him too much at the moment.

Besides, there was something else he needed to do. Jackson got back on his laptop and went back to *R.I.P. to my brother Kevin.* He went to the end of the thread and just rested his fingers on his keyboard for the longest time. Finally, he typed *Kevin won't be forgotten.* Then he hit ENTER, joining the mourners.

Almost immediately, he got a message from Anna. *What are you doing?* his cousin asked. *You didn't even know him.*

She was right. Jackson deleted her message and then deleted his comment about Kevin. He shut his laptop down.

After that, he tried lying on his bed to finish rereading *Watchmen,* but every other panel, his mind wandered.

He wasn't any more focused when he moved on to the Xbox. It turned out that, compared to those activities, picking up books and bath towels and dried-milk glasses was relatively easy to do while thinking about some dead guy. By the time his mom got home to take Jackson to afternoon practice, he'd done everything on the list. Except actually turn on the dryer.

Grouped with the offensive and defensive linemen, as promised, Jackson could see that even with the height he'd put on since the spring, he was only in the middle of the pack sizewise. Maybe closer to the bottom third. He definitely wasn't one of the favored players, but at the moment that just meant he could observe the more experienced guys doing the drills before he had to do them himself.

Had Kevin played football? If he'd still been in high school, would his teammates be doing the whole black-armband memorial thing for him this season? Would—?

"You're up, Deets! Four-point stance! When you see my hand move, that's the way you roll!"

On the whistle of the coach facing him, Jackson dropped to all fours. When the coach's hand to his left moved, Jackson fell to his stomach and rolled over once in that direction. He lay there in the practice field's bristly green grass, waiting for the next hand movement, but the coach seemed to be waiting for something, too.

"Deets, get *up*! Four-point stance!"

By the time Jackson got the hang of the drill—attempting something a dozen times in fifteen seconds gives you a pretty good sense of what you're supposed to do—it was another player's turn. Jackson jogged to the back of the line, where he stood and tried to brush off the bits of grass clinging to his sweaty forearms, without much success.

The coach next led the linemen off the field to a telephone pole lying on the ground and framed on either side by a strip of dry, packed dirt. Jackson heard him say something about fingertips just before demonstrating a pole-straddling bear crawl. "Remember: tips of the fingers." Then the coach blasted his whistle, and the players in front of Jackson began cheering on the first guy in line.

Could Kevin have possibly pictured this scene? Not this drill, not this practice itself, but him, Jackson, thinking about him, Kevin? Before Kevin decided to end his own life, could he ever have imagined the ripple effect it would have? The thoughts and comments and conversations that would result? The fact that, two weeks later, some kid he'd never met, practicing football all the way down in Texas, would be thinking about Kevin, the fact that he'd lived and the way that he'd died? Would knowing all that—?

"DEETS!" A whistle shrieked in his ear, accompanied by an echoey slap to his helmet. "Look alive! *Go!*"

The first player to bear-crawl the length of the pole

had looked like he'd been shot from a cannon. Maybe the next eight or ten had, too—Jackson couldn't say. But Jackson felt like he was just lumbering along. The palms of his hands hit the hard dirt with a thud, and with his legs spread to avoid starting a splinter collection in his inner thighs, he moved forward his left foot, then his right. He pulled up his arms and pretty much just fell forward, catching himself with the heels of his palms before his face mask bashed into the pole. *Time for the feet again,* Jackson thought.

Would knowing all that have made any difference to Kevin? Would he have still—?

Jackson felt the tearing sensation in each hand at the same moment. His palms both skidded a bit when they came into contact with the cracked ground, and then they began to burn and sting. He could hear another player thundering and grunting behind him, and Jackson knew that—face mask or not—falling onto the pole would only hurt worse. *Fingertips,* he remembered, and he finished the drill with his fingers spidered out and the heels of his hands as far from the dirt as possible.

When he got to the end of the pole, Jackson used his recently honed rolling-over skills to bring himself to a sitting position, from which he rose without using his hands. He was almost afraid to look at them. He turned his palms up and saw that on each, the outer layer—two outer layers? three?—of flesh on the heels had been ripped away, with dirt and bits of dried Bermuda grass sticking to the blood.

"Coach?" Jackson said.

One of the student managers led Jackson to the break area and turned on a spigot. Jackson winced as the water hit his palms. "We'll get you cleaned up more in a bit," the kid said as he unsnapped Jackson's helmet and took it off. "Coach says go ahead and get yourself something to drink." Then he ran back toward the practice field.

There were three coolers, each nearly as long as Jackson was tall. He used a knee to open the nearest one. It was filled with ice and Gatorade. Jackson grabbed an orange-flavored one and let the cooler lid drop. He was just about to twist the cap off the bottle when he remembered he had no flesh on the part of either hand that would come into direct contact with the cap. Even without twisting it open, that would hurt like hell.

He opened his mouth wide to fit around the cap, thinking he could twist it off with his teeth, but that just made his jaw ache.

So Jackson waited.

A few minutes later, the entire team took a break and hustled over to where Jackson stood waiting with his hands stuck out and a bottle tucked under his arm. Everyone's first priority was getting himself something to drink. Jackson could relate.

Rangy was the first to notice him. "Yow!" he drawled

as he saw Jackson's hands. "You didn't stay up on your fingertips, did you?"

Before Jackson could answer, Rangy grabbed the bottle from under his arm. "Let me open that for you," he said, removing the cap with an ease that Jackson thought he'd never again take for granted. "Here."

"Thanks . . ." Jackson's voice trailed off at the point where he would have used Rangy's real name if he'd known it.

"Kevin," Rangy said. "You're Jackson, right?"

Jackson nodded. He took the bottle in both hands, holding it where his fingers met the undamaged upper parts of his palms. He closed his eyes, tilted his head back, and began drinking the whole thing down.

"Welcome to the team, Jackson."

I HAVE A GUN

WILL WEAVER

THE PHONE JANGLED. Lydia Nicholas, eighteen, looked up from her book but didn't move. It was her mom's phone, the one with a tangled black cord and old-school answering machine; its calls had nothing to do with Lydia. But her mother and grandmother were gone to Mass, and the phone kept ringing. Eight times, actually, before the answering machine clanked alive.

Lydia mimicked her mother's voice: "This is Rosemary Nicholas. We're not home. . . ." For God's sake, why not just say, "Leave your number"? This was the 21st century. People knew what to do. Why belabor the obvious? Or how about a phone message with the truth: *None of the Nicholas family is freaking home right now—literally or otherwise. Don't leave your name and number, because no one will get back to you. We don't give a shit. We have our own problems.*

"This is Sergeant Benilli at the Queens Village precinct station."

Lydia yanked off her earbuds and sat up. She heard herself suck in a breath. *Please, please, no more bad news.*

"We have closed out our paperwork on the shooting incident at your house and we have some personal effects ready to release back to you. You may have a family representative pick them up anytime from the station. Please bring proper identification."

She let out a breath and stared across at the answering machine and its now-blinking light. Her sudden worry (*a random shooter at church? a taxi crash?*) for her mother, and grandmother, who was still living with them four months after Kevin's funeral, washed away before a sudden high curl of rage.

"'Effects'?" she shouted at the blinking light. "Fucking *effects*? No 'Sorry for your loss'? No 'You have our deepest condolences'?"

Heartbeat thudding in her ears, she turned back to her College Algebra I book. She took night classes at Queensborough Community College, and real numbers were just beginning to make sense. Now her train of thought was gone. She took a long breath and read the passage again: *Real numbers are points on an infinitely long line where the points are equally spaced. An irrational number is a real number that cannot be written as a simple fraction, and so is missing from the line.*

An irrational number.

Missing from the line.

"Like Kevin," she whispered. Her only brother, Kevin.

She grunted against a spasm of grief inside her and clutched her rib cage. They came less often now, but anything, even algebra, could trigger one—a slosh of stomach bile flooding into the space where Kevin used to live. A breathless, suffocating feeling. When they passed, she never felt any better, just empty. Kevin was a fuckup, but still he was her only brother.

She got up and walked over to the phone. Beside the little table was a coatrack with one of her mother's scarves, gray cashmere, dangling limply. She reached out and touched the soft wool. Drew it to her face and smelled her mother's hair, a scent like walnuts. Her mom was not a perfume kind of woman. Lydia had never even seen her wear lipstick since her father had died, also by suicide.

She looked down at the answering machine. One of the reasons her mother kept the old mini-cassette player was that their father's voice was still there, in the messages, a ghost in the machine, but real if anyone wanted to hear it. She knew Kevin had listened to it sometimes when he was really stoned. She had caught him once, sitting splay-legged on the floor, punching the buttons over and over and just staring at nothing. What a fucked-up family she had.

Suddenly the thud of a car door—and then another—came from the street. She peeked past the side of the curtain. A taxi with her mom and grandmother had arrived home from church. Quickly, urgently, as if her life depended upon it—hurry!—she punched the rewind arrow. The tape whirred and clicked as she deleted Sergeant Benilli's message.

"We're home!" her mother called from the foyer.

Lydia had managed to arrange herself on the couch exactly as before. Black hoodie zipped all the way up, its comforting hood flopped halfway down her forehead.

"Yes, I can tell," Lydia said flatly.

"Did you get some work done, dear?" her grandmother asked, completely missing the sarcasm. The two women were dressed in dark raincoats but bright scarves; Lydia could smell fresh air on them.

"Sort of," Lydia said, looking up briefly. Her grandma and her mother were always on a cheerfulness high after Mass, but church was like a drug: it always wore off. By supper time they'd be faking it. By eight p.m. they'd be silent and withdrawn. By nine p.m. they'd be gone to bed in their separate rooms.

The next day at the police station in Queens Village, she handed over her cell phone to the uniformed black woman who sat by the metal detector, then waited as the woman dug briefly through Lydia's backpack and gave her a once-over: *medium-height girl with short black hair; jeans, hoodie, and a backpack; no face metal, piercings, or visible tats: no threat here.*

"Okay," the guard said, and nodded Lydia forward.

Lydia stepped through the doorway-like frame without a beep, then approached a counter that said INFORMATION. Everybody uniformed worked behind glass, and the glass had a fine mesh of wire in it. She spoke into a little microphone.

"Second floor," the man said.

The retrieval office was staffed by an older cop with a very gray face, as if he had not been outside for years.

"I'm looking for Sergeant Benilli?" Lydia said. She handed over her driver's license.

"That's me."

"My family got a call. We're supposed to pick up some effects that were my brother's."

Officer Benilli read her license.

"Kevin Nicholas?" Lydia added.

"Yes, of course," he said. He looked up from her license. "I'm so sorry for your loss."

Lydia swallowed. She could only look down at the officer's hand that held her license; at his fingers, which were stubby but straight; at his clean, straightly clipped fingernails.

"Usually it's the parents—" the officer began.

"I'm the family representative," Lydia said, cutting him off. "My father's dead and my mother, well, she's not doing so well these days. This is something I can do for her." She held full eye contact with the cop.

"And you're eighteen?" the officer said, looking down again at her license.

Lydia waited. *Do the math.*

He nodded and handed back her license. "All right, then. Follow me."

A buzzer hummed, and he held open the wire-screened door. Lydia followed him down a hall to a room with a wall of small lockers. With a key, he opened number 27.

Lydia sucked in a sharp breath. *Fuck me!* The handgun lay inside—the gun Kevin had used to kill himself. What had she thought "effects" meant? How could she not have thought of this—that it was the gun? She heard herself mouth-breathing.

"Are you sure—?" the officer began.

She took a breath. "Yes," she said. "I'm good."

Around the pistol lay a scattering of stubby, brass-colored bullets. The arrangement looked like a metallic alien insect with babies. Opening the locker—letting light in—might disturb the nest; any second now they would stir and hiss.

"After all, it has to be done, right?" she added, trying

109

to sound totally adult—as if they both understood the dark humor of the moment.

"Not really," the officer replied.

Lydia looked his way.

"Here's how it works," the cop explained. "After any kind of fatality involving a firearm, we secure the scene, the county coroner does his report, and afterward—when it's clear that no foul play was involved, and that the gun has no history—well, we have no reason to keep it. Which is why we called you."

Lydia stared. "No history?"

"It was a legally purchased firearm and has not been involved in any sort of crime."

"Okay," she said.

"However, we would be happy to dispose of the gun for you," the officer said. "Very happy, in fact. From our point of view, it would be one less gun out there."

She touched the butt of the gun with one finger. *The last thing my brother touched.*

"I understand," she said. "But I'll take it."

"Okay, then." The officer picked up the pistol. Keeping the dark eye of the muzzle pointed at the floor, he squeezed a button; the clip dropped from the handle. "Empty," he said, and set the clip aside. Then he worked the pistol's slide action with a sharp, metallic *shhhh-clack!* He put one eye closer to the back end of the barrel, where the bullet would come up from the clip. "And chamber empty."

"Thanks," Lydia said. Stupidly.

"Do you know anything about guns?" the cop said, not ready to hand it over.

Lydia shrugged. "Not really."

"Well, it's empty now, and I'd suggest keeping it that way. Remember: it's not a toy."

And I'm not freaking thirteen.

Three minutes later, Lydia was back outside the station with her backpack hanging heavily from her shoulders. It was amazing how dense—how heavy—a handgun was. She straightened her shoulders and headed toward the bus stop. There was a line, and by instinct she hurried to get in it, but, almost there, she jerked to a halt. What about packing a gun on a city bus? An older black woman in line stared evenly at her. Lydia averted her eyes and walked quickly on.

She walked a couple of blocks, then caught a cab. Settled into the stale-smelling back seat. The driver waited. He looked at her in the mirror. "I drive, but I not read minds," he said.

"Sorry," Lydia said. She swallowed, then said, "Eternal Rest Funeral Home. Off Springfield Boulevard."

At the tidy, low building, with its perfect shrubbery, the parking lot was empty; at least there wasn't a funeral today. She paid the driver, and as she got out of the cab, brass cartridges clinked inside her backpack. The cabbie gave her a wide-eyed look, then drove off abruptly with a chirp of his tires.

The front door to Eternal Rest was open. To the side, the chapel area was totally empty. Farther down the hall, loud hip-hop music played from an office. Someone laughed, a hearty guffaw. Maybe that older guy, Sampson. Party time at Eternal Rest. Clearly no dead to wake up.

She approached the open door. Inside was a small group of people: Sampson, the smooth-talking front man; his assistant, big dude Morris Something, a guy she sort of recognized from school; and a pretty woman with the styled hair of a beautician. The three were having coffee and eating donuts.

Sampson saw her first and jumped to his feet.

"Sorry! We didn't hear you come in," he said, quickly standing up and coming to meet her. It was as if he wanted to block her view of the office, its life, its warmth, its music. "Turn down that goddamn music, Morris," he barked over his shoulder. He closed the door partway and stood before her. He was dressed in jeans and a white lab-type coat with a couple of splotches on it that she tried not to look at. "How can I help you, miss?"

She held the backpack in front of her. He clearly didn't recognize her. Inside the office, the music died, and then Morris looked out through the half-open door. He blinked, then his face brightened.

"Hey!" he said, and stepped out. "Lydia, right?"

Sampson looked at Morris with surprise.

"Yes. Lydia Nicholas," she answered.

"Morris Adler," Morris said. "So nice to see you again."

"Ah, sort of," Lydia said.

"Lydia, of course," Sampson said quickly. "You look . . . different today—better," he added, touching her arm and holding on to it briefly. The perfect gesture of warmth. Of condolence. And no small hint that she was not un-pretty. "How are things with you and your family?"

She paused. "I have a gun," she blurted out.

"Whoa!" Morris exclaimed, and ducked behind Sampson, whose back stiffened. His eyes went to her hands, which clutched the backpack.

Behind Morris, in the office, there was silence. Inside, the attractive woman stared at Lydia with unblinking eyes, her fingers poised over her cell phone.

"I mean, a gun in my bag! My brother Kevin's gun. I'm not, you know, like a crazy shooter!" Lydia said.

"Okay," Sampson said evenly.

"I just don't know what to do with it." Her voice broke at the very end.

"Yes, I see," Sampson said in a measured counselor's type of voice. He eased closer—shape-shifted, almost—to take hold of her backpack. She let go of it. Gave it over to him.

All eyes went to the backpack.

"I just picked it up from the police station," Lydia continued. "The cops called and said to pick up his effects, so I did—I didn't want my mom to have to do it—but now I have his gun." And then, disgustingly, she leaned against the wall and began to weep.

"Nadira, would you excuse us?" Sampson said.

Nadira nodded. She paused by Lydia to give her a one-armed hug. "You came to the right place, honey."

"And Morris, don't you have something to do?" Sampson asked.

"Ah, not really," Morris replied with a round-eyed, innocent look.

Sampson looked greatly annoyed. "Okay, let's all just relax a bit. Please, come—sit down," he said, guiding Lydia forward.

Morris stared at the backpack. Sampson carefully unzipped it. He reached inside and, careful to keep the muzzle pointed away, withdrew the pistol.

"Ruger forty-five caliber," he murmured, as if confirming some piece of a puzzle. "I guessed as much." He quickly turned to Lydia. "Sorry," he said. "You didn't need to hear that."

She stared. "It's not like I didn't see what it did to him," she said. She wiped at her eyes, more pissed off at crying than anything else.

Morris handed her a fresh tissue. "It's all right to cry," he said. The phrase sounded practiced, rehearsed, part of his job at the funeral home.

"So what do you intend to do with the gun?" Sampson asked.

Lydia shrugged. "I have no fucking idea."

Sampson leaned back as if to think. "Do you mind?" he said, then turned up the radio again and punched it to a different station, one that played jazz.

"This place gets kind of dead at times, if you know what I mean, so we play music," Morris said to Lydia; he waited expectantly to see if Lydia got the joke.

"Jesus, Morris! Who put a dollar in you today?" Sampson said.

"Sorry," Morris said with a hangdog look.

Lydia's mouth twitched; she looked away to keep from laughing.

"*Any*way," Sampson said, "you now own a gun. One that has some family history."

Lydia stared at the black weapon.

"Which means you have some options," Sampson said.

Lydia waited.

"You could throw the thing in the river," Sampson said, holding the gun up to look at it and turning it toward the overhead light, "which I'd hate to see because it's such a nice piece."

She was silent.

"You could sell it," he continued, "but who knows what happens to it then."

Lydia waited.

"Or," Sampson said, turning to her, "you could keep it and learn how to shoot it."

Lydia's gaze went to the pistol. "Why would I want to *shoot* it?"

"Because if you keep it, you need to understand it. Be comfortable with it. If you don't get to know it— if you're afraid of it, or angry at it, or you blame it for Kevin's death—then it's gonna always be, like, radio-active. Like a dead mouse in the closet. It's always going to smell."

She stared at the gun. Sampson held it out to her, handgrip first. She took it. Let her fingers close around its butt. The cool heft, the way the curve fit the valley of her thumb and forefinger—it was like suddenly having a third elbow or wrist or hand. The weight of it had a kind of current that struck all the way down through her belly to her toes. "How would I learn how to shoot it?" Lydia asked.

Sampson shrugged. "We're a full-service funeral home," he said.

■ ■ ■

At home that night, she cooked for her mother. It was their favorite family dinner, pasta with anchovies.

"This is so nice of you," her mother gushed. "I could have—"

"Sure you could have cooked," Lydia said, "but I wanted to, okay?"

She met Sampson at the Leaf Haven Pistol & Rifle Range on Jamaica Avenue, which was only a few minutes from Queens Village and on the bus line. The parking lot was long on pickups and SUVs. Most had National Rifle Association bumper stickers or SUPPORT OUR TROOPS magnetic ribbons.

"Hey!" Sampson said, spotting her. "Ready to rock?" He carried a duffel bag.

Inside, they signed in. The clerk, a guy wearing yellow-tinted glasses, greeted Sampson by name, then moved his eyes up and down Lydia.

"I'm a member," Sampson said to Lydia. To the guy he said, "Guest shooter today."

"Always happy to see a new lady shooter," the guy said with a wink to Lydia.

Below the floor came dull *poom-poom* and thudding noises, like a percussion group tuning its equipment. There was a smell, too, with a slight bite to it, like smoke from an electric range on its high-heat oven-cleaning cycle.

"Sign this," the clerk said.

When she finished, the clerk said, "Now, be careful down there, honey."

Lydia didn't reply. When they were out of earshot on the stairs heading down, Sampson said, "That guy says that every time to everybody. 'Be careful down there.' Annoys the shit out of me."

"He kinda has a point," Lydia murmured as the shooting sounds grew louder.

Sampson draped his arm over her shoulders. "Don't worry—I learned my shooting in the army," he said. "Three tours in Iraq."

She hesitated before the steel door.

"I have earmuffs for you, and safety glasses," Sampson said, wiggling his duffel bag. "Everything we need."

The narrow shooting lanes, each protected from the others, were slightly claustrophobic, but less so when she focused on the gun in Sampson's hands. And then hers. He made her go through a safe pistol-handling routine a dozen times before loading the gun.

"I'll shoot it once first, then it's your turn," he said.

She nodded and put her hands to her ears.

Sampson stared.

"Duh," she said as she touched the round earmuffs already in place.

"Here we go," Sampson said.

Lydia squinted.

He turned, steadied his outstretched arm, and fired.

It was not that loud, sort of like someone bouncing a basketball once, sharply, on a wooden floor.

"Now your turn," Sampson said.

He stood close behind her—she could smell his aftershave, or maybe it was only facial soap—and steadied her outstretched arms with his longer ones. His torso was against hers, sort of like dirty dancing. But with a gun in her hand.

"Nice and easy: squeeze."

The pistol bucked in her hand. The recoil struck through her wrist, arm, and trunk like a really good swing of a softball bat—that aluminum *clank!* of perfect contact.

"Good," Sampson said.

A full clip later, she was on her own. The target was the small black silhouette of a man. Or maybe just a small black man, who grew more tattered and invisible with every shot.

Sampson gathered up the empty cartridges. "Souvenir brass," he said.

"Okay," she said.

He put them in a side pocket of her backpack. "You're a natural," Sampson said as they headed back upstairs.

"Not sure about that," she said. In the lobby there was brighter light outside the window; the sun had come out. It was as if the world had turned a notch.

"We'll need some ammo for next time," Sampson said to the clerk. "A box of .45 ACP."

"What's ACP?" she asked. Now that she had shot the pistol, she felt weirdly free to ask questions, even dumb ones.

"Automatic Colt Pistol," the clerk said as he reached under the counter. "Gotta keep your bullets straight, okay, honey?"

"My treat," Sampson said. He paid for them, then handed the box to her.

As the front door closed behind them, Lydia glanced back. "That guy was creepy."

"But now you don't have to worry about creeps, do you?" Sampson said. His eyes went to the box of shells in her hand and to her backpack.

"I guess not," she said.

There was a long moment of dead airspace. "Look," Sampson said, "do you need a ride somewhere?"

She paused, then shrugged. "I was going to take the bus."

"With what you're carrying, you'd better not," he said.

"Yeah. I thought of that."

He pointed to a nearby SUV, and they headed that way. "Guns are complicated," he said as they walked. "Everything changes when you start packing. You start doing things you shouldn't be doing. You walk down streets you shouldn't be walking down. You go to parties you shouldn't be going to —"

"Hey, I'm a big girl," she said.

He looked sideways; his eyes went up and down her. "Here we are," he said, and unlocked the Jeep Cherokee.

She got in. The interior had leather seats and smelled like cigarettes, but it was not messy.

"Where can I take you?"

"Home. I live up on two hundred and seventeenth. Near the library."

He turned at the light. They drove along in silence for a while. "Hey, are you hungry or anything?" he asked.

She was silent a moment. "Maybe."

"Maybe?"

She shrugged. "Yes."

"There's an ice-cream place on Hollis."

She nodded. "All right. As long as you don't get creepy on me."

He grinned. He had very nice teeth. "Hey, I'm thirty-four. You're, what, nineteen? Maybe twenty?"

"Twenty," she lied.

"So that settles that," Sampson said. He looked over at her.

When she didn't reply, he concentrated on his driving.

At the small and crowded ice-cream shop, they

shared a small table, New York style, with a couple her age. They had backpacks, too, and looked vaguely familiar, as if they might be students at QCC. But they were in love and didn't so much as look at Sampson and her.

His thigh pressed against hers underneath the table. She didn't move it. They took their time. Talked some. A little about Kevin. A little about Iraq. But back in the car they lurched toward each other and in seconds were kissing. Hard, even painful kissing. His hands were all over her breasts—she let him—and then one went to her crotch, which she arched toward him. The only thing that saved them from getting arrested for public indecency was the console and the gearshift between them.

And it was Sampson who suddenly pulled free. "Sorry!" he said quickly. "I don't know what I was thinking."

"Don't worry about it," she said. She touched his face.

"I need to take you home, right now," Sampson said.

"Okay," Lydia said easily.

He let her out at the corner. After he drove off, she slung her backpack over her shoulder. Inside, the brass cartridges tinkled again, like tiny wind chimes from a sudden breeze. As if weather—maybe a storm of some kind—was moving in.

CONNECTIONS

MARINA BUDHOS

THE DAY OF my friend Kevin's wake, I put on my brand-new suit—the same one that's for my sister's confirmation.

Except that Kevin wasn't really my friend. And my sister isn't my sister. Not by a mile. Not any day soon.

I'm not being coy here. Not at all. Kevin was some guy I met in accounting class at York College. We both were, let's say, taking the slow lane in college. Checking out a few classes here and there, heading for the exit ramp before the first assignment was due. Snatching grins at the back of the class. Both business majors, but who knows what that means. When the lady at registration asked me to pick a major, I just checked a box. It sounded good. Something that would get my father off my back.

Oh, yeah. Papi. Another almost-connection. The guy who hauled off from Costa Rica when I was two, got himself some good jobs working crew for some Bangladeshis who renovated fancy brownstones in Brooklyn. Then one of them set up a trucking company at JFK Airport and made him inventory manager. My mother used to cash his checks at the *farmacia* and fold the bills in a flour jar at the back of the shelf, until I caught on. He sent postcards, birthday cards, checks for extra English classes, a package of Mets jerseys and shorts that puckered too tight against my legs.

And the photos: Papi sitting in a backyard, his belly like a heavy rising moon, a scraggle of a beard around his chin. "Oh, looking so old," Mami whispered. She had given herself to him when she was sixteen, and I think she believed that's what they still were—sweethearts fingering each other's new and surprised selves, doing all the wrong things at night in the soft mud of the coffee-bean fields; young newlyweds in her parents' front room, she with a silver ring on her finger, he with a jaw shaved stubble-raw, a plane ticket to New York in his new denim jacket. Papi standing proud and upright in front of his beige-brick office in a uniform, his hair thinned and blowing up off his scalp, a thick fish of a gut sloping over his leather belt.

When I turned fifteen and Mami was sick of me stealing from the flour jar, sick of me running in the streets, she began to pester him. *It's time. Your son. Tu hijo. You promised.*

So he sent for me. Dude's got a nice tidy three-bedroom house in Queens Village, owns it even. A Weber barbecue on the concrete patio, freezer chock-full of dark, slender-necked *cervezas*.

And get this?

We ease up to the curb that first day, when I'm groggy and stiff from the frosted whoosh of plane air—my first and only plane ride—and lump chicken in a plastic tub, and the front door swings open. Out stumbles some six-, seven-year-old boy shouting, *"Hermano! Hermano!"* And then the other by the doorjamb, my half sister, Alicia, quivering thin and guarded as a greyhound, turning an icy cheek as I step up and try to give her a hug.

Yeah, dude's got another family.

Funny how he didn't mention that all those years. Ma kept working in the bakery, sliding those huge stainless-steel pans of buns and quivering flan, combing the buttery flakes from her long hair every night and winding the strands up tight again like a dark and shining secret, a knob of pain. I think she knew. That's why, whenever I asked, "What about this Christmas? Is Papi coming?" she shook her head. Or the time I listened to her talk for a long time on an overseas call; after, I heard her sucking down her sad noises in her room.

In ten seconds the story shears off like a cliff edge,

125

not a word said. It all makes sense now: Papi's hollow slap on my shoulder when I stepped through the airport gate. The frozen bracket of his mouth. The thump and tumble of my heart as we stood next to each other at the baggage claim, a rigid silence between us. Okay, you haven't seen your father for thirteen years; it isn't like some warm head nuzzle in his armpit will change all that. He isn't your father. Not really. He's just some guy. Some Yankee-made-good with a green Nissan, air freshener spinning on the rearview mirror, and a wife, standing shy and awkward down the hall at the kitchen counter.

My father's wife's hair is dyed an improbable shade of gold-yellow. Her jeans, the seams studded with mirrored sequins, make huge half-moons of her butt. Neither of us knows what to say. I even feel sorry for her. I feel sorry for both of us. She's folding meat on a platter. I'm stuck at the doorway, sniffing. I've never seen meat like that — white-pink as the underside of a pig's belly. No bristle, no bone, just smooth as a plastic tongue. A chemical stink, like the air freshener in the car, sweats off the meat, comes spinning up my nostrils.

Soon I'm all elbows and heaving motion as I stagger across the linoleum. "Over here!" she cries, and that makes it even worse — they've got a bathroom, with a tiny sink with taps like gold nuggets, and even this makes me sick. Then I'm heaving a bitter taste all over the guest towels.

"Looking sharp!" Benny exclaims, glancing up from his bowl of Frosted Flakes. His eyes are two appreciative, shiny brown pennies. He shows a jagged set of baby and grown-in teeth, which give him a goofy, half-finished look. We share a bedroom, and the adoring waves Benny sends over sometimes ease me up.

But Papi's all scowls. "You can't go."

"What do you mean?"

"You can't. It's your sister's confirmation."

He still calls her that. Alicia's half. Not even half, since for almost all of my life I didn't know she existed, that she lived in a room with one wall painted a pink so neon-bright it hurts my eyes, that she had Dora the Explorer parties where Papi twisted balloons for the kids. A whole story detonated itself minutes after I walked into his house three years ago. And I'm *still* picking out the bits from my innards. That counts for something, doesn't it?

"It's a wake," I tell him.

"What's the matter, they don't have other hours?"

"No."

Actually I'm not sure. I got the notice off Facebook. Some friend of a friend who posted. *R.I.P. Kevin.*

Come pay your respects at Eternal Rest Funeral Home. I don't care. No way Fish Gut is telling me when or where I have to be.

"You get back here—"

Fat chance, I think, edging down the hall, nearly knocking over the flower arrangement that's sheathed in crackling plastic. This whole house billows with Alicia's confirmation. Pink streamers draped in the front entrance, platters lined up on the counters. I go into the bathroom, and there's some satin and silk confection hanging on the shower rod, and my stepmother is telling me not to touch it because the dress has to "air."

Now the door swings open and my stepmother steps into the hall, shopping bags tilted on her wrists. Alicia is right behind her. Her hair has just been done at the hairdresser's, and it swings in a shiny wave at her shoulders. Her face is buffed smooth with makeup—no betraying rot of acne today.

"Got yourself dolled up," I comment.

"Yes," she whimper-smiles.

"What'd they do? Sandpaper your cheeks?"

Her mouth wobbles.

"Must you?" my stepmother pleads. I can hear my father cursing in the kitchen.

It's all I can do to push past the two of them.

■　■　■

Guilt's a heavy pivot between me and my stepmother, and I crank it on her bad. Every time I step into a room, I see her mouth collapse and her eyes draw down like shades of mourning. She acts stupid and clumsy around me—and she is: too young to be my mother, too afraid to take it out on Papi for never hauling out the truth. And so I never take out the trash or wipe the mirror after a hefty shower. I finish up Alicia's last Diet Coke and put the empty bottle back in the refrigerator door. I ask for a five here, a ten there for pocket money, even though Papi told her, "Let that lazy ass get himself a job."

I made her buy me this suit. Told her I needed it because I was a business major. That I had interviews, lots of interviews. And it was Kevin who made me do it.

This suit is fine, with thin lapels and tailored pants that drape just right over my loafers. *Very* GQ *sly,* Kevin would say. It's not like anything I've ever owned. But I needed her to do this for me—to watch her swipe her plastic card, bang it by the register, and rack up tens, hundreds of dollars I know she can't afford. A mean and sour fog settles in my chest when I think of my stepmother.

That's how me and Kevin first got together—he had a way of knowing what I wanted, before even I knew.

In accounting class we were supposed to break up into pairs and go over our homework. When the professor paused for a bathroom break, Kevin gave me a nod, and I gathered my backpack and slipped outside with him.

"You want a cigarette?" he asked.

"That's okay. I don't smoke."

He looked hurt for some reason. I could tell right away, he was one of those guys who just wanted to give stuff away, as if it embarrassed him to have anything. We sat on a low wall, our heels bouncing against the brick, and he dug out his cigarette and drew on it for a while.

"I didn't do the assignment," he explained. "And I didn't want that girl next to me giving me a hard time."

"Me neither," I said.

"I know." He offered a loose, sloppy grin.

"I don't even have the textbook," I added.

Here his head bobbed up. I saw the pupils of his eyes contract. They made a weird purple color, almost fluorescent. "How come?"

I shrugged. "Spent it on a new phone."

I pulled the phone out of my pocket. I'd already put on a blue rubber skin, loaded it up with all kinds of stuff—Temple Run, iFunny, Flashlight. Showed my little brother, but no one else since they'd all know how I bought it.

Kevin admired it for a long time. He tested its sleek heft in his palm, checked out a few of the apps, sweeping his fingers on the screen. All the while he asked me questions: "How long you been here?" "Where you live?" "With who?" "They know you don't go to class?" I told him everything. About coming up here three years ago. How nothing I do ever adds up the way it was supposed to. I said nothing about my stepmother, swallowed her down like a dark potion. I don't know why I told Kev so much. He seemed to get it, though. He took in each notch of my story as if he had heard it before. When he handed me back the phone, I noticed how our wrists were the same tawny color, same width.

Then he said, "I know how to get your textbook."

By the time I get to the bus stop, I can hardly breathe. I've run the whole way there, and it's only when I scramble up onto my seat that I notice I still have a tag stitched to the cuff of my suit sleeve. "Don't rip it," I can hear my stepmother say. "Let me use the needle."

Of course I stepped away from her. "I can take care of it," I mumbled.

Now I'm staring at this cheesy bit of cardboard by my wrist. I don't even know what I'm wearing this sucker for anyway.

A few days ago, Papi told Alicia that no boys could come to the party tonight, not even from catechism class, and she hurled a hairbrush at the wall, nicking the wallpaper. I thought for sure he was going to explode, slide the belt out, but instead he shook his head, laughing, and walked away. "Women's nerves," he muttered.

That's what gets me.

I could never throw a brush. Kick up a scene. I'm walking a fine line between boarder and street kid they've let in on probation. Papi's patience with me burns short and harsh as a cigarette stub. But give him Alicia and he's soft and jolly. He even goes to her teacher conferences, shyly palming his hair down before heading out in the Nissan. My stepmother, she was born here, just a few blocks away in Queens Village. She was the one with money for the down payment for this house. So Papi is always working hard to show her he's level with her. No slippage marrying the Costa Rican who never got past eighth grade.

I know all this. But it doesn't make it any easier, I think, as I start to gnaw away at the threads with my teeth. Doesn't get rid of the scooped-out hole in my chest. The hurt, down deep in my marrow somewhere, that Mami is some kind of a shadow, a fearful smudge on an X-ray he wishes would go away.

That day after accounting class, when Kevin and I walked into the college bookstore, a girl behind the counter grinned at him and came hurrying out. "Kev! How are you? We miss you."

She had a body like a low-necked bottle, heavy at the bottom. The clipboard made her a little more efficient-official, not just your run-of-the mill work-study cashier. She had to stand on her toes to hug him, 'cause Kevin was one big guy — thick, meaty shoulders; a slightly dopey, bashed-in mug; and fierce, pained eyes. Kind of like a dog who'd been trashed and let go on the streets.

Kevin chatted her up good. Natalie, her name was. I watched their hips bumping, just so, as they talked. Tiny flush marks, like sleep puckers, showed on her cheekbones.

"You miss me so much," he teased, "why not give me Friday shifts again?"

She looked at him sharply. "You know I can't." She glanced around, suddenly nervous. "You better go now. George will be back from his lunch break."

"Nat—" His big hand rested on her side, just by her ribs. Something told me that wasn't the first time his hand had made it there.

"This is my buddy here . . ." He tilted his head toward me. Then he managed to edge her toward the back room. The cashier, the real one, rolled her eyes at me.

A few minutes later, the two of them emerged. Natalie's flush had spread up over her ears around pale almond skin. Then we headed right past the scowling cashier, through the front door, with a brand-new accounting textbook, still in its plastic skin, setting off no alarms.

"What was that about?" I asked, as we reached the street. "You used to work there?"

"Yeah."

"What happened?"

"Lots."

■ ■ ■

It was always the same with Kevin. A nod, a lift of his chin, that fierce poison swimming up from behind his eyes. We sprang out of York College like hungry, roving street dogs. I couldn't figure him out. He seemed to know everyone—greeting guys in the halls, the food court, the library, with high fives, slaps, and intricate finger signals, but he was always alone. Never stopped moving with that big, loping body of his, never explained himself.

Usually we stopped off to see someone, almost always a girl—got ourselves a freebie, a Coke, a sub. Once we took the subway to a corner outside FIT, where a friend sold shawls and scarves to the pretty fashionistas that wiggled by. Kev made his friend hand me a scarf—a gold-russet one with silky fringes. "Give it to your stepmom," he said. "Put it between you."

I folded the scarf into my bureau drawer that night. Never did give it to her.

I don't know why he picked me. Maybe the Papi connection. Told me his dad came from Puerto Rico, married a white lady, disappeared a long time ago.

"She even changed our last name," he said once, laughing. "That's why I'm Nicholas."

"Ooh, that hurts," I said.

"Damn right it does."

Beyond that I didn't know much more. He didn't live at home anymore, though I wasn't sure where he parked himself. Had a sister, a year younger. Kev always wore long-sleeved shirts — I can say that, buttoned up to his neck and wrists.

That's what he was wearing on a sweltering October day when we were in — of all places — Roosevelt Field, the shopping mall. Kev looked terrible. I hadn't seen him for weeks and weeks, and he looked drawn down, wasted. His skin was the color of water-stained Sheetrock. He gave off a stale smell — something crumbling dustily inside. In the men's department, he kept browsing, fingers tapping thin strips of shiny belts, ribbed socks, shoes — not like the kind anyone I knew would wear. "Nice stuff, no?" He grinned. "You ever know someone get in a suit like this? Go to work that way?" I noticed rims of dirt under his nails.

Then he made me try on the suits. At first I protested, but you don't say no to Kev. He brought them out — armloads — even called out one of the salesmen, whose eyes went narrow, but then Kevin explained I had a bunch of interviews lined up for internships, and my sister's confirmation besides.

Kev was in a different area, eyeballing suits seven hundred, eight hundred a pop. "Kevin, I can't!" I whispered.

He didn't listen. He made the guy unlock those beauts and slide them right off the clacking wood hangers. Boy, that shit felt good. Like putting my arms into a cloud. Some dude brushing me down, making me step up on the platform, tucking and nicking here and there. Nobody ever did that for me before. And it worked: I saw myself a thousand times over in the three-way mirror. I saw shoulders and a collar, the lean angle of a waist. I saw me walking right through glass. Striding off the tarmac, steam blowing right up my pant legs like a big man. Showing Mami it wasn't a mistake. *I* wasn't a mistake.

"Awesome," Kev said. He set his big hands on my shoulders, spun me around. The tag twinkled. Eight hundred ninety-five.

"Make your stepmother buy that for you."

"Why?"

"Just do."

His gaze stayed on me, like a wan electric current. He looked sicker than ever. His cheekbones seemed to quiver. "You make people show what you are to them," he added. "Make them *pay.*"

As I watched the salesman slide on the plastic cover, I felt a raw hunger scrape up against my ribs. Like nothing I'd felt since I'd come north. Nothing I'd ever known. I wanted everything. I wanted the suit, I wanted to get back to school, I wanted to make good on my life. I could have eaten those shirts and ties and shoes.

Then I turned around and realized Kevin was gone.

I can see the sign for the Eternal Rest Funeral Home from the bus stop. It's a short walk over, the only real house on a block of low brick commercial fronts, red shingles with a peeling, white-banistered porch. A worn strip of green outdoor carpet arrows down the stairs and across the pavement to the curb, where the cars are still pulling up. For once I wish I smoked. I squint at the various people pushing through the doors, try to see if I recognize anyone. Then I tug on my jacket, swallow a few times. I check my watch for about the fiftieth time.

That hot afternoon at the mall, I found Kev outside, leaned up against a car, flashing a bleary grin. A security guard scooted us along—a guy probably not much older than either of us, just doing his job.

We collapsed onto a strip of hedged grass, at the end of the parking lot. Kevin flung himself down. The sun needled down hard. Still he wore that crazy flannel shirt buttoned to his wrists. He looked worse than before. A shade of fear tapped my heart. Was he sick?

"Hey," I ribbed. "Why don't you take that thing off?"

"Shut up," he snapped. But he was sweating like crazy, so he did strip off his shirt, and that's when I saw it—the scar on a tender stretch of his forearm. My stomach did a little quiver. I could just make out the letters, shiny white beads stitched on the skin: *SC*.

Sweat streamed off him now, glazed him in a pale hue. His hair was plastered thick as gum on his forehead.

"He just went and offed himself, you know," he whispered.

"Who?"

Then I felt stupid. What a thickhead I am sometimes. I didn't make a move, a sound. All the molecules in the air gathered around Kevin. He glittered. He shone. It was the most he ever said. Not that it was much. Just what I hadn't seen before. The hole his father disappeared into. The phone call from the police in the middle of the night. His mother wasn't even sure how they had her number, it had been so many years. An ocean of broken glass beneath his skin.

He turned. "You ever think about that?"

"What?"

But I knew what he meant. I just couldn't get a word up through my throat. I was plugged deep with terror.

He slapped the grass, gathered up his shirt. The scar letters glinted on his arm. "Forget it. You got a lot to look forward to, man. That's why you got to get that suit."

Next thing I know, dude's running across the lot. For a sick guy, he hauled over that fence something quick.

Two days later, I got the news. An update came floating to the top banner on my new phone. I swept my fingers on the screen, widened the little bubble of letters. Read it again. The air around my eyes buzzed. I couldn't even feel my own fingertips. Realized it was the girl

Natalie, from the bookstore, who posted first. *WT—?*
she'd scrawled.

The guy who stands at the front of the funeral parlor,
instructing people to sign the guest book, looks about
my age. Kind of chubby, an overgrown kid squeezed into
a dress shirt and tie, not commanding and somber, as he
should be in a place like this.

Then a girl approaches me—she has the same eyes as
Kev, the same tawny skin.

"You're a friend?"

I nod, feeling like a fraud. I shouldn't even be here.
"From York College."

She cracks a rueful smile. "Sometimes he went to
classes." Pointing to the casket, she steps aside. "Please,
go ahead. They did a great job."

"Nadira," someone pipes up from behind.

We both turn, puzzled. It's the pudgy guy, looking
flushed and pleased, squeezing his fingers in front. "She's
our cosmetologist."

"Yeah, right," Kevin's sister says, a snarl in her voice.

I don't blame her. Who boasts about the makeup girl
at a time like this?

"Get back to your book," I hiss to Mr. Upbeat.

The last thing I want to do is make a move toward
that casket. I hang back behind a skinny girl weeping so

hard she's carrying a whole tissue box under her arm. Her extravagance annoys me. Kind of like Alicia. Everything done up like some stupid housewife reality show. Keep it chill, Kev would say.

Before I know it, I'm right up front on the line, staring down at a rubber-faced guy who once was Kev. I can see the clay edge of makeup where they folded his dark hair over his cheek.

"That's one beautiful suit," I murmur. And it is: the fabric's made of some finely dyed wool — slate blue with tiny bits of darker blue. The lapels angle down clean, even with him lying straight out. He looks slick as can be, *GQ* sly.

"He picked it out."

To my surprise, his sister has stayed by my elbow. She shakes her head. "Don't know how he did it, but he scraped the money together and bought it. Had it spread out on a chair, right where they—" She looks away.

"When did he . . . ?"

She's still talking with her face turned, so I can see only her trembling profile. "For two days, he didn't answer his phone. He shut himself into his place. No one heard from him."

I feel as if the whole room, the ceiling, has crashed right down on my head.

I was nothing. But I was the last.

The one who helped him pick his burial suit.

It all makes sense: that day at the mall, sprawled out on the grass, Kev sweating, sick as a dog. He was talking not to me, but to himself. All I complained about, my family, my stepmother and half sister, it wasn't the same. Maybe I wanted it to be the same, but it wasn't. My papi is a two-timing liar who can't even own up to what he did, but he didn't off himself. Didn't put the cold muzzle of a gun to his mouth. Didn't leave a crater growing hairy and big as a cancer inside.

I walk the whole way back to the church, all forty blocks, clouds scudding loose and jumbly overhead. It's as if I never breathed the whole time I was in that funeral parlor and this is the only way I'm ever going to get air inside me again.

"Why didn't you tell me?" I hiss at Papi.

He looks at me, puzzled. "About what?"

I make a face, nod toward Alicia and Benny, who are following my stepmother through the huge doorway. She's wearing a brand-new silk dress, and it makes a shushing sound against her stockinged thighs. "About them."

He hesitates. "I couldn't."

"Why?"

He rubs his palm back and forth on the back of his neck.

"I was scared, *hijo*. That's why."

This is the most conversation that we've had in three years.

We step into the church, where the organ is sounding out. I slide down next to Alicia on the pew. She smells of shampoo, tangy apple. I lean over and do something I've never done before. I kiss my sister on the top of her hair. She looks up at me, puzzled. Then her little furrow of anger gives way to surprise. She grins, taps her shoes together. She's just a girl, I realize. A little girl.

I never bought that eight-hundred-ninety-five-dollar suit. Instead I let my stepmother take me to the Queens Mall. And it wasn't such a bad day, either. She zigzagged her way from the parking lot, up the escalators, into Macy's. She knew her way around that place, for sure. She guided me right past the crappy suits for old men, right to the snappy Calvin Klein and Hugo Boss ones on sale. She jerked the salesman around, too, told him how to hem the pants, just so, next evening if you please. It was the first time we'd been alone, the first time I let a complete stranger know that we were connected. At the cashier's, she touched the rim of the credit card to my cheek, crisp as a blade, and whispered, "You don't tell your father, okay? You deserve it. You'll get a job. I know you will."

The priest steps up to the front. His vestments, two bands of red and yellow, gleam on his chest. He lifts his fingers, and all the girls and boys, including Alicia, file up the aisle. Everyone seems to have taken a breath, waiting. We can feel it. Me too. My arms, my shoulders, even my legs.

We can all tell something's about to begin.

AFTERWORD

MARC ARONSON

Charles and I had a blast working with our team of authors putting together *Pick-Up Game,* a cross between an anthology and a novel. What could we do next? We—and, we hope, readers—especially enjoyed the braid, as individual stories written by different authors shifted characters and story lines, making each one both a piece in itself and part of a larger whole. How else could we use that format? *Pick-Up Game* was set in one spot, the West 4th Street basketball courts in Manhattan, on one day. Could we find a new weave with a new challenge?

Charles knew, almost at once, where to go next: initiation. The word comes from the Latin for "to begin," but it can also carry the meaning of "to go through the proper rite or ceremony to be admitted into a group, or to become a member of a secret society." So much of being a teenager is about crossing lines, reaching a new status or standing, and gaining previously hidden knowledge, whether that is in the socially sanctioned steps of communion, bar/bat mitzvah, quinceañera, or graduation; the intimate bonds of friendship, secrets, and sexuality; or the dark vows of gangs, guns, and crime. You could fairly define all of teenage as a sequence of initiations dreamed about, yearned for, accomplished, regretted, found marvelous, found disappointing, found life-changing, passed, all the way along. We had a theme. Now, how to use that theme in our weave of authors?

We turned to Rita to start us off, and she cleverly and carefully laid out her lines, giving enough character and setting for other authors to explore, all around a funeral home and a corpse. Death would start the life of this book. We didn't know where the authors would take the stories. Their instructions were to link, in some way, to the first story and to work with the theme of initiation. The wonder of the process was how their stories built and how two key characters began to emerge: Kevin, and, well, I'll leave you to decide the other. Before photographers had digital cameras, they used film, and the negatives had to be developed in a darkroom, where they went through various chemical baths. As the sheet of images emerged, you began to see, for the first time, what the photo would look like printed. That's what this book was like: slowly characters and stories, linked but separate, began to reveal themselves.

But it wasn't easy. We owe a big—no, a huge—shout-out to our authors, who accepted the kaleidoscopic nature of creating a book like this. Each new story slightly—or significantly—changed the others. That sent ripples all through the chain, even back to Rita's first story. And then as she and others revised, changes rippled through once again, and again. We were so grateful to the authors who went back, and back, and back again to iron out the creases and tie the book together. And this went beyond lonely revisions; authors began sending notes to each other, being extra sets of eyes or guiding hands, helping build our joint book, helping weave the braid we'd envisioned from the start.

But where would it end? Where does a novel that begins with a death and weaves through many dark initiations go? Marina's story answered that for us. We were thrilled: our novel-in-stories had the true arc of initiation, of transformation, of change, hard-won. And perhaps on another level, that is what this book meant for all of us: we know the initiations of being a teenager can be terrifying as well as thrilling and can have the most extreme consequences. Every author, I sensed, had a personal need to honor young people finding their way, negotiating choices, deciding which lines to cross.

It can be okay, they seemed to want to say, even when for now it is not. Because ultimately what the initiate gains is knowledge, wisdom about the world and its ways. The Norse god Odin gave up an eye to gain wisdom. In a sense we all do. This is a novel-in-short-stories about the bargains we make to cross lines, to join in, to be accepted, to begin to know, at whatever cost, who we are. Scarred—no, graced—with the knowledge we have earned, the next phase of our lives begins.

ABOUT THE CONTRIBUTORS

MARC ARONSON enjoyed working with Charles and all of the authors on this book. He began his career in books for younger readers working as an editor and finds the weave between writing his own books and working on the writing of others ever challenging and ever fascinating. He is now a full-time faculty member at the School of Communication and Information at Rutgers University.

CHRIS BARTON grew up in Texas, lives there still, and knows about those telephone poles and two-a-days from personal experience. He won a Sibert Honor for *The Day-Glo Brothers*. His extensive knowledge of putting up false fronts comes (mostly) from researching and writing the young adult nonfiction thriller *Can I See Your I.D.? True Stories of False Identities*.

NORA RALEIGH BASKIN is the author of ten novels for young readers. She has won several awards, including a Schneider Family Book Award for *Anything But Typical*. A 2001 *Publishers Weekly* "Flying Start" selectee, Nora Raleigh Baskin has also published short stories and personal narrative essays that have appeared in the *Boston Globe* magazine and *The Writer* magazine. She teaches creative writing at schools and libraries across the country, as well as through the Gotham Writers' Workshop and the Hudson Valley Writers' Center. Her most recent young adult novel is *Subway Love*.

Nora's story is yet another iteration of her own autobiographical history given to a fictional character from a childhood of dysfunctional memories. In other words: the gift that keeps on giving.

MARINA BUDHOS grew up in Queens, a setting she revisited while researching her nonfiction book *REMIX: Conversations with Immigrant Teenagers* and her award-winning young adult novel *Ask Me No Questions*. She is currently working on an adult novel, a second nonfiction book co-written with Marc Aronson, and a young adult novel that was inspired in part by the voice and characters she created for her story, "Connections."

ELLEN HOPKINS is the award-winning author of ten *New York Times* best-selling young adult novels-in-verse, including *Crank,* plus two adult verse novels. She lives near Carson City, Nevada, where she recently founded Ventana Sierra, a nonprofit organization that helps youth in need obtain safe housing and assists them in working toward career goals through higher education, mentorship, and the arts.

A.S. KING is an award-winning author of young adult books, including the highly acclaimed *Reality Boy,* the *Los Angeles Times* Book Prize winner *Ask the Passengers,* the Michael L. Printz Honor Book *Please Ignore Vera Dietz, Everybody Sees the Ants,* and the upcoming *Glory O'Brien's History of the Future.* Her short fiction for adults has been widely published and nominated for *Best New American Voices.* After fifteen years teaching literacy to adults in Ireland, she now lives in Pennsylvania.

TORREY MALDONADO was voted a 2012 Top 10 New Latino Author to Watch (and Read) by LatinoStories.com. His debut young adult novel, *Secret Saturdays,* was an American Library Association Quick Pick and has been featured on CNN and other media outlets. Praised for its current feel and timeless themes, *Secret Saturdays* has found a place on both state and college reading lists alongside classics. Born and raised in a Brooklyn project, Torrey overcame neighborhood poverty and violence to be the first member of his immediate family to attend college. A graduate of Vassar College and veteran teacher, Torrey also trained schools to implement conflict resolution programs through the country's largest victim-services agency.

CHARLES R. SMITH JR. is the author and photographer of more than twenty books for children. He has won numerous awards, including a Coretta Scott King Author Honor for *Twelve Rounds to Glory: The Story of Muhammad Ali* and a Coretta Scott King Illustrator Award for *My People.* He has shown his versatility with a novel, short-story collections, poetry, biography, and nonfiction. This is his second anthology as an editor and contributor. His first, *Pick-Up Game,* was also co-edited with Marc Aronson. Charles R. Smith Jr. lives in Poughkeepsie with his wife and their three kids.

WILL WEAVER'S novel *Memory Boy* is read widely in schools across America. An outdoorsman from Minnesota, he owns several long guns for hunting. His most recent book is a memoir, *The Last Hunter: An American Family Album.*

RITA WILLIAMS-GARCIA is the *New York Times* best-selling author of nine novels for young adults and middle-grade readers. Her recent novels *Jumped* and *One Crazy Summer* were named National Book Award Finalists, and *One Crazy Summer* was also named a Coretta Scott King Author Award winner, a Newbery Honor Book, and a Scott O'Dell Award winner. Her short stories have appeared in more than a dozen anthologies, and she sponsors an annual short-story writing contest for teens. Rita Williams-Garcia lives in Jamaica, New York; has two adult daughters; and is on faculty at the Vermont College of Fine Arts Writing for Children and Young Adults MFA Program.